T0208791

Other Books by Patricia Apelt

The Melrose Farm Series

Circumstantial Connections

Green Mountain Mysteries and Ship Shadows

Coming soon:
The Empires Series

Four Leaf Clover
and
The Luckiest Man
Alive

PATRICIA APELT

ARCHWAY PUBLISHING

Archway Publishing books may be ordered through booksellers or by contacting:

Archway Publishing
1663 Liberty Drive
Bloomington, IN 47403
www.archwaypublishing.com
844-669-3957

ISBN: 978-1-6657-3231-4 (sc)
ISBN: 978-1-6657-3229-1 (hc)
ISBN: 978-1-6657-3230-7 (e)

Library of Congress Control Number: 2022919803

Print information available on the last page.

Archway Publishing rev. date: 10/25/2022

This one is for the biggest supporter other than my family.
Here's to you, Patricia Darby.
Thanks for the memories, the fun shopping trips,
and the tea parties. I will miss you.

Acknowledgments

As always, my special thanks to my biggest support
team. Daughters Kathleen Apelt, Wendy Apelt
Matheson, and Laura Apelt Maney, and the males in
my life, husband Walter and sons John and Charles.
And a big thanks to my Beta readers Linda Hartmann,
Pat Darby, Joy Reszek, and Kathleen Apelt. Also,
a special thanks to my "Technical Advisor"
Ed Hartmann.

Once again, to all of you, your critical comments,
positive and negative, helped me prepare
this work for publication.

Chapter One

SEBASTIAN JAMES COLE SIGHED in contentment as he lowered himself into the lawn chair and carefully put his cold beer down on the stone floor of the cave where the family picnic was in full swing. Known as "King" to friends, family, and close business associates, he was well pleased with what he saw as he looked around the large area. Digging into the mounded-over food on his plate, he had to smile at his wife Abbi and their twins Larona and Loren. They were just outside the cave entrance enjoying a dip in the kiddie pool, along with his sister Katie, and her little Susan, while Katie's husband Russell and Susan's Great-Uncle George Montgomery proudly looked on. The Mayhew's had recently been able to adopt Susan after rescuing her from a flooded river, then finding that her parents had drowned in that raging flood. During the adoption process they had also discovered she had no living relatives except "Uncle George". Having no children of his own, he was very happy to visit her as often as possible and was now considered one of the family.

King's long-time friend Will Brackston, his wife Melissa, and Granny Edi soon joined King, closely followed by Jeff and Samantha Barlow. Granny Edith Melrose Bradley had raised her grandson Will here on this farm since his parents had been killed in an automobile accident when he was just a young boy. Because of the various happenings in their lives that brought all the young people together here at Melrose Farm, Granny Edi now thought of all of them as her Grandchildren and they all thought of each other as brothers and sisters. It was a close group, and they enjoyed getting together as often as possible. Thus, the picnic in the Green Mountain cave.

Granny Edi, after finally accepting that Will was actually very happy being an archeologist and had no wish to be a farmer, had divided Melrose Farm into three separate properties and given them to her "adopted" grandchildren. Jeff and Sam were given the land on one side of the farmhouse, Will and Meli the original farmhouse and the central section, and Russell and Katie the other one-third, which included the old dairy barn and pasture. Russell and his construction crews had turned the huge barn building into office space for the joint Cole-Mayhew Construction Company on one end of the first floor, with a garage on the other end, which also included "Katie's Kennels" where she raised and trained golden retrievers as Companion Dogs. He had built out the loft as living quarters for his family that also included an apartment for the Coles whenever they could fly in from their home in Texas.

Both the Mayhew section and the land now belonging to the Barlow's had lovely tall mountains at the back. Katie had named the Mayhew side Green Mountain and the recent discovery of a tunnel system, and this cave had prompted the upgrade from just a really large cave into what Will called a "Summer Kitchen". Since the main tunnel was entered from the basement recreation room of his farmhouse, running both into Green Mountain and into Sam and Jeff's "Crystal Cave" on the other side, Will had suggested they all be cleaned of dirt and cobwebs and lighted so they could be used for the many family gatherings. It was easy to now go from his house to either this big cave or the smaller ones in what was soon to be Sam and Jeff's home.

As she took her seat in the circle Sam spoke to Meli in a loud whisper. "That baby of yours looks just like her Daddy! Strangely, despite how ugly Will is, she is adorable!"

"I heard that. Sis!" Will said as he picked up his bottle from the floor. "But I have to agree with you about how adorable Maddie is."

Madeline Louise Brackston had been named after Meli's Mother and the aunt who had raised Melissa after her mother's death. Aunt Louise and her husband David were now over in the "nursery/playroom" area of the big cave, holding and humming to Maddie. Standing beside them was Doctor Clifford Simmons, a widower and long-time friend of the family. He also was the brother-in-law of Granny Edi, having married her twin sister, Clarissa years ago. She and their unborn child had died in the same accident that took Will's parents. Doc Simmons gently put his hand on Maddie's head, gave a few slow caresses, and then watched as Louise slowly put the sleeping baby down in the Port-a-crib. All three adults then walked over to the buffet lunch spread out on the rock ledges along the back wall, filled their plates, then joined the others.

Chapter Two

HEARING HIS WIFE CALL him, King put his plate down next to his beer, stood up and headed outside, grabbing several of the large dry towels stacked on one of the nearby picnic tables as he went by. When he got to the pool Abbi was already lifting Ren out, so he held his arms out to Rona and she hurled herself at him, soaking his shirt in the process. He was able to juggle her into one arm, toss a towel to Abbi and one to Katie for Susan, and wrap his daughter in another, all while listening closely as Rona told him about the lizard they had just seen running across the rocky path.

Russell and Uncle George followed Katie and little Susan back into the cave/party room just as they all heard the first rumble of thunder. Russell quickly pulled the big glass door closed and said to King, "I'm very glad you suggested adding this door. We could not have had the use of the cave as often without it. Before we put it in, almost every time there was a storm, the wind blew right into most of this space."

King said, "Just glad I had already put one in my own home, so I knew the right people to call. I think my living room at Castle Rock wouldn't have been very comfortable if they had not figured out how to attach the glass to the stone walls. They used the same process to put in all my windows too, but you don't have that problem here."

Another conversation grabbed their attention.

"I have, and I think I have about decided to take you up on it!"

"What are you suggesting now, Clifford?" Granny Edi was sitting right next to him so had overheard the conversation. "Trying to get George into trouble with another one of your schemes?"

George laughed, then said, "Not at all, Edith. He has just been telling me how much he enjoys living at the retirement home and is suggesting I give up my rooms at the hotel where I live now and come be his neighbor. I just need to find out if you have an apartment available where I will have easy access for my wheelchair. I'll need at least three bedrooms. I still need an office for my work and my driver, Phil, wants to come with me, so that means a bedroom for him."

Russell spoke up to say, "Indeed, we have a three-bedroom unit available. All the units we just completed are on the ground floor of the new section and are completely handicap accessible, and they all have their own entrance out to the new deck. From there, you can go down a ramp for complete access to all the grounds, which includes a smooth path over to Doc's clinic and bungalow. You two could visit as often as you like."

Having filled their plates and picked up a beverage of choice, the rest of the group joined King at the picnic tables. Putting her plate down next to Russell, Sam asked him if he had had a chance to talk to his other partner, Si Nobles.

"Yes, we talked briefly two days ago." Russell answered. "He said to tell you he will come here to talk with us next week. You and Will need to have all your questions handy, and sketches of what you want the house to look like. You guys have decided you want it mostly outside of the mountain, right?"

"Yes, that's right. We want to take advantage of the connecting tunnels, of course, plus the little pond and Crystal Cave, but not too much more of the other caves and tunnels. There is too much beauty in all the formations. We don't want to damage any of them. We'd like to use some of them for storage and hallways, but not as everyday living space. So, I guess most of the house would sort of wrap around the side of the mountain."

"I agree with you on that, Sam." King turned to speak to them, and continued with another comment. "My 'castle' home is another kind of rock altogether, so it doesn't have the stalactites and stalagmites found in your tunnels and caves. It really would be a shame to have them destroyed. I think Si can come up with a design that will take advantage of some of them, but not be a threat."

As he was saying the last words, his cell phone rang, so he excused himself and turned away to answer it. Not recognizing the number, he answered rather formally, "Hello, Sebastian Cole here."

"Hello, King. This is Megan Marshal from the Circle M. I hope I didn't catch you at a bad time."

Turning toward his sister, King, smiled as he said rather loudly, "Metal-mouth Megan? It's been a while."

At that, Katie came running over to where he was sitting and pulled the phone down so she could speak into it.

"Megan, is it really you? Gosh, how long has it been?"

"Katie? Oh, it's so wonderful to talk to both of you at once! And it obviously hasn't been long enough for that brother of yours to forget that horrible nickname. But those ugly 'tooth-fixers' are long gone, and I'll forgive him if he will do the favor I called to ask about."

"Oh, right, you did call to talk to him, so I'd better give the phone back. But we need to stay in touch. Bye for now."

As Katie handed the phone back to King, she said to the others, "That is an old friend of mine from when we were children. Her parents own the ranch next to ours and we played together all the time back then. We were always getting into trouble together. She has a couple of older brothers just like me, and the boys thought it was great fun to torment us. But all of us had great times together too. I haven't talked to her since we finished college and she went off to Europe for a couple of years. Wonder why she is calling King?"

Abbi asked, "Does she still live with her parents? Maybe King and I could ask her over sometime."

Having finished his conversation with Megan, King spoke up. "I'm glad to hear that, Love, because I just invited her to visit as soon as we get back home. It seems she has a big construction project she wants my advice on."

"Did she say what it was? Are they adding something to the Circle M?", Katie asked. "I can't imagine what they would need help with there if it's just another barn or something."

"All she would say at this point was that is had nothing to do with the ranch, and that it was too involved to get into over the phone. I guess we will have to wait until we get back to Texas."

Sam asked, "When do you plan to leave? Not too soon, I hope. You've only been here a few days."

"And we can stay a few days longer, but I have a meeting next week about another project I'm working on. We should probably think about leaving the day after tomorrow, so I have time to gather my thoughts and drawings well before the meeting."

"As much as I hate to bring it up," Louise said, "all this talk about leaving reminds me that David and I need to get back on the road if we want to reach home tonight. Meli, it has been such a wonderful thrill to see your beautiful Maddie and thank you again for thinking of both your mother and me when you named her. I know Madeline would have been so proud."

"Thank YOU, Aunt Louise. And you two, Uncle David. I was so fortunate to have you two take me in when Mama died. Please come back to visit us often. Come on and I'll drive you up to the house while Maddie is still asleep."

Saying their goodbyes to everyone and thanking them again for lunch, Louise and David put up their umbrellas and hurried through the door to follow Meli down the path to where the four-wheel all-terrain vehicle was parked. It wasn't a long drive through the pasture and up to the farmhouse where their car was parked, but the bad weather would have made it a very unpleasant walk. Meli pulled up as close to their car as she could, gave each of them a last hug, waved them off, then headed back to the mountain cave and the rest of the party.

By the time she got back, everyone had finished eating and the ladies were cleaning up the trash and putting the leftover food into the refrigerated chest to be carried back to the farmhouse. The babies were still sleeping, so all the adults got another bottle of their favorite beverage and settled in for a cozy chat, guys at one table and gals at another. Pretty soon, Edith began to nod her head.

Sam said to her, "Granny Edi, would you like me to take you back so you can take your afternoon nap in your room?"

Edith roused enough to agree, and started getting up from her chair, telling everyone to come back to the house and stay long enough to enjoy some of her peach pie. Then she and Sam headed for the "back door" of the cave. Jeff got up and started to follow. He told the others, "I'm going too. I need to get to the hospital to check on a patient. Last one out, remember to drive the 4-wheel back. With this rain it will be a lot dryer walking through the tunnels, but we don't want to leave the car behind."

The others waved them on, so Jeff followed his wife and Granny Edi through the door and down the ramp into the tunnel. Granny Edi was saying, "You know you do not really have to leave the party just to escort me back to the house. With these handrails you boys put in, I'm able to manage just fine. I might be blind as a bat, but these rails are all I need to guide me back to the house. I have done it before, you know."

Sam took the hand that was not on the rail bolted into the wall of the tunnel. Then she said, "It's not your blindness that concerns me going through these tunnels and you know it. You do so well at everything you try, I never even give a thought to the fact you can't see. But with all this rain we have been having lately, I am afraid the floor will be slippery with dampness, and you will stumble. We can't have you falling in here all by yourself. Besides, I have to work on the house plans we need for Si."

Jeff spoke up to say, "I have a few new ideas for them too. Why don't you work on the plans for the kitchen and your office while I'm at the hospital, and we can both tackle the rest when I get home."

"Great! Maybe we can actually have them all finished before Si comes over."

Granny Edi asked, "So, Sam, have you figured out how you will get all the light you wanted into your kitchen? Building the house right up against the mountain will block all of one side, but you said yesterday you thought you had solved the problem."

"Yes, I think maybe my idea will work. I just must sketch it out on paper to be sure. Careful now. We're at the other ramp. It should not be damp at all, being on this end of the tunnel, but hold on just to be sure."

"Yes, Mother."

"Smarty!" Sam opened the door into the basement recreation room of the farmhouse. "And your welcoming committee is here to greet you. All three of them! Sorry you were not invited to the party this time, guys, but we felt it would be a bit crowed with you there. Next time, I promise."

The golden retriever, Prince, had gotten down from his favorite chair to meet them at the door. Charlie the cat and Cisco the monkey were just stretching and getting down off the top of the bookcase built along the opposite wall. The old chair in the corner and the plump pillows on the bookcase were there just for the spoiled animals, and they took full advantage of them.

With Prince leading the way, they all walked over to the elevator and rode up to the first floor. Jeff gave Sam a quick kiss on the cheek, picked up his medical bag and light jacket from the table by the door, and left. Granny Edi turned toward her bedroom at the back of the house with all the animals following closely behind. Sam shook her head at the four of them as they went down the hall, then went into the kitchen and on to the back door. Her office was out by the garage, so she grabbed her raincoat hanging on the rack by the door.

Chapter Three

BACK OUT IN THE cave-turned-into-party room, the groups had shifted around somewhat, but there was still a lot of joking and conversations going on. During a lull in the talk, George turned to Will and said, "I understand you are the one that found this cave. Care to tell me how that happened?"

Will smiled and said, "I fell into it!"

"What!" George exclaimed.

"Well, not exactly into the cave, but into the tunnel. You see, Russell and I were trying to remove an ancient furnace out of the basement of the farmhouse. I got behind it to push it away from the wall, and instead, I went backward through the wall. Turned out, it was through a long-forgotten door leading into the tunnel system we now use to get here to the cave. After we all explored it thoroughly, we found the tunnels not only connect this cave with the farmhouse, but with Sam and Jeff's mountain as well. We can go back that way if you like. The tunnels are wide enough for your wheelchair and we covered the steps at each end with ramps to make it easier for Granny to use that route rather than being driven through the pasture as you were today."

"That is an amazing story!", George said. "What was the purpose of all these tunnels?"

"Judging by the apparent age of the digging scrapes and markings and using my archeologic knowledge to make a guess, we think they were put in when this property was first settled as an escape from Indian attacks. That would be several centuries ago. We also found ledgers here in this cave that were filled out during the time the tunnels were first dug and then more when both the tunnels and cave were used as part of the Underground Railroad. None of us have had time to examine them yet, but we hope to do that and write a book on the contents."

"Oh, I would very much like to help with that! Is there anything I can do?" George seemed really excited about the prospect. So much so that Russell asked, "Uncle George, some time back during one of your visits to our Susan, you and I got into a discussion about what you did before you joined the military. Didn't you tell me you were a college level Professor of History?"

"Why, yes. I spent six years teaching History on the college level just before I enlisted. I guess that is why I'm so excited about your ledgers."

Russell thought for a few minutes, gazed around at the others, then faced George again. "The eight of us that discovered the ledgers, plus Granny Edi of course, made an agreement to vote on anything having to do with how they were to be handled. I'm not sure, but I think the vote might be to let YOU read them and write up a summary to be turned into a book. None of us really have the time to devote to it and do it justice." Looking around at the others, he continued,

"I would have to talk to Sam, Jeff, and Granny Edi, but with your qualifications, I don't see a problem with letting you take this project off our shoulders, do you guys?"

There was a round of "Yes!", and "Great idea!", and "Glad you thought of that." Katie came over and put her arm around George and said, "Oh, Uncle George, this would be wonderful. And it gives you another excuse to see your Great niece. Susan will enjoy that!"

"Super!" King said, "but for now, let's table this discussion. The rain has stopped, and I hear our two munchkins waking up. Let's get everyone back to the house so we can talk further."

Abbi agreed, and said "How about you guys clearing away the tables and chairs while we gals get the babies changed and ready to go?"

Meli said "If one of you gentlemen would please take the cooler out to the four-wheel, I'll drive that back and let Will push Maddie in her stroller through the tunnel. She loves watching all the lights."

The tables were soon wiped off and arranged back along the wall, with the benches and lawn chairs wiped down and stored neatly on top of them. George commented that it was a very organized 'withdrawal exercise', and clearly had been done many times. Meli grabbed the trash bags and left through the sliding doors at the entrance to the cave and almost skipped down the short path to the four-wheel. Will closed and turned the several locks on both sides of the door and pulled the drape closed.

George asked "Why do you need to lock the doors? Surely only family comes here!"

King answered, "You haven't been to my house yet, or you would know the answer to that. You see, both my house and this cave have the front doors set into rock walls. No matter how hard we try, we can't seem to find a way to completely seal them from rain blowing in unless we lock them tightly to compress the gaskets around the edges."

"Well, that seems like an easy way to handle it. Now, show me those tunnels!"

"O.K.! Everybody ready? Doc, why don't you lead, then you, George, and the rest of us will follow with the babies. Last one out, please turn off the lights."

It was a slow parade because George had to stop often to ask questions and absorb what he was seeing. When they reached the tunnel leading to Sam and Jeff's Mountain, Doc Simmons, George, and Will with Maddie went several feet into the storage room at the entrance while the others scooted around them and continued to the house. George exclaimed over the rail they had installed for Granny, and the continuous line of bright lights put in mostly for Meli. Will explained about his wife's horrible accident that had left her blind for several months and still a bit wary of dark places.

"Even with all these lights on, she would still rather drive the four-wheel than come this way." Will told him. "She is getting better and will come this way sometimes, so we don't say anything about her driving whenever she volunteers."

Continuing in the main tunnel, they soon came out into the Recreation room, and then on to the elevator. It was not quite big enough for all of them plus the wheelchair, so George, King, and Abbie with their twins went up first. Katie took Susan and Doc. Simmons on a detour into the pantry closet to grab a couple of jars of green beans for dinner. Will stayed behind to shut off the air conditioning and make sure the T.V. and all the lights were off. They all met at the elevator and went up together.

Once settled in the living room, the ladies gave bottles to any baby wanting one and the guys settled back with their feet up on hassocks and sighs of contentment. About that time, Granny Edi came out of her room and went to her favorite chair, Prince settling at her feet and the other two animals jumping up onto "their" window seat.

George spoke up to say, "I'm learning so much about my new family today, but I haven't yet heard the story of all your pets. Anyone care to enlighten me?"

They all laughed, then Katie said, "Well, to start with the easiest one, Prince was one of my companion dog studs and training aid for Katie's Kennel until he got too old to help me train the young pups. I gave him to my brother, then King brought him here to help Granny Edi when she was recovering from her broken leg.

"Charlie is a pedigreed Flame Point Himalayan Persian and has won several ribbons at shows. He belonged to my aunt until her female cat turned against him, and wouldn't tolerate him anywhere near her, so Auntie gave him to Sam and me. Meli, you're up."

"Ah, yes. As you know, Uncle George, I am a Photojournalist. I was on assignment in Asia, and at the end of it my guide gave me Cisco as a thank you for my trouble. I think he was not so much a 'Thank you' as just a way to get rid of the silly creature. Now all three of them have latched on to Granny Edi and don't even acknowledge the rest of us are here most of the time."

Granny said, "Oh, they know you are here when it's feeding time! And speaking of feeding, has everybody's lunch settled enough to enjoy a piece of that pie I mentioned earlier?"

Sam got up and said, "I think that's my cue! And I hear Jeff coming in just in time to join us. O.K., coffee and pie coming up!", and headed toward the kitchen, the other three young ladies right behind her.

With cups of coffee at their elbows and huge slices of pie on their plates, they all settled more comfortably into the couches and chairs scattered around the large room. After finishing about half of his pie, Russell spoke up. "Sam, Jeff, and Granny Edi, a conversation came up out in the Summer Kitchen after you left. One that I think you might be interested in." Waving his hand around the room to include the rest of the group, he continued, "We started talking about how the tunnels and the cave were re-discovered, and the ledgers we found there. I remembered something Uncle George had told me, and we would like to share that with you. He told me that he taught college level History before joining the military. Using his knowledge of how History books should be formatted, he would like to help us with the task of reading and summarizing those journals into book form, if that would meet with the approval of everyone. Time to think about it until the pie is gone."

Once all the plates were empty and coffee cups in hand, Russel said, "O.K. Show of hands!"

Coffee cups were shifted into one hand and the other one raised. All but one.

"O.K., Meli, what is your objection?"

"Nothing was mentioned about using all those photos I have already taken and written captions for!"

George practically shouted, "You have relative photo documentation for all this?"

"Well, yes. Thank goodness, we realized what a treasure we had found before any of it was cleaned and history destroyed in the process. I took lots of shots of the whole tunnel system, the cave, and the ledgers before the guys brought in the power washers to get rid of all the dirt."

George very quietly said, "Saints preserve us. This is the chance of a lifetime! Excuse me while I faint dead away!"

Everyone chuckled, then he added, "Meli, I think it's now time to "mention" those photos and captions and ask politely for your permission to use them in the book. Not that we need to ask your permission, since that was the reason you took them in the first place, correct?"

"Yes, writing a book was the intent from the beginning, and if it is a collaborative endeavor, I'll raise my hand to vote with the rest! When can you start?"

"Whoa!" Give me a minute here. Russell, you said there is a three-bedroom apartment available now? How soon could I move in?"

"Give the paint about three days to dry thoroughly, then move in any time."

"Great! That will give me plenty of time to get back to the hotel, pack up my few possessions, and close out my affairs up there. My current apartment is rented furnished, so I will need to pick up new things when I get back. A bed for starters, as I have my own chair! Then I will fill in more things later.

As soon as I have a place to lay my head at night, I can start on the book."

Doc said, "If you really want to speed things along, why don't you think about bunking with me until you can buy furniture? There is even an extra room in the clinic where your driver can sleep for a few days."

"That would be super, Cliff. I would still like to put off working on the ledgers until Tolleson and I are settled in our own space. Those books have waited a couple of centuries so a few more days will not matter, and it would be safer not to move them around too much. We would not want to take a chance on losing anything. Speaking Tolleson's name must have conjured him up! I hear him out on the driveway now. I have truly enjoyed my day here so much. Thank you again for including me in your family."

Katie and Russell got up to walk out with him. Katie put Susan into her uncle's lap, and Russell pushed the wheelchair down the ramp off the back porch. Tolleson came over to say 'Hello' and give Susan a tickle under her chubby chin. Katie took the baby while he helped George get into the car. Russell folded the wheelchair and stowed it in the trunk, then stood by Katie and waved as the car rolled away. They could see that George was talking non-stop to his driver as they pulled out onto the road in front of the house.

Chapter Four

THE REST OF THE week and into the weekend was quiet, with Jeff going to the hospital as usual, Katie working with her golden retrievers while Sam watched Susan, and the others going about their normal business. In the evenings, they all enjoyed gathering in the living room for dessert and coffee and good conversation. On Sunday evening, King and Abbi told them that they had to leave the next morning to fly back to Texas.

Will drove them to the airport and helped load the twins and all their luggage into the Mayhew-Cole corporate jet. King and Russell had purchased it for their joint construction business and King flew back and forth between the homes frequently. He and Russell always conferred on their many projects when he was in town, so there was no problem saying he was using it for "business use". The fact that Abbi and the twins joined him on his business trips was not an issue.

The Coles had an uneventful flight and arrived in Texas just before lunch. King had left their car in his hanger at the local airport, so he and Abbi quickly transferred the babies and luggage, and soon arrived home to what was locally known as "King's Castle."

Having taken advantage of a natural sandstone tower riddled with tunnels and caves, King had turned it into a comfortable home. Called Castle Rock for centuries by the Spanish settlers of the region, King's great-grandparents had named Castle Ranch after the popular name for the formation. King, Katie, and their brother Bob had played in the tower often when they were children, then the two youngest had stopped coming once their lives had gone in different directions. Once grown, King had decided he wanted to live there instead of at the main house with his brother or build a conventional house somewhere on the ranch. Enlarging some of the caves in the tower, smoothing the floors in the tunnels, and bringing in all the water lines and electrical wires had been a monumental task but had resulted in a wonderfully comfortable home.

Because of everything that had to be offloaded and taken into the house, King drove up to the driveway turnaround on a huge ledge just outside the front door. He and Abbi each took a baby into the house and settled them into the playpen, then went back for the rest. Setting down the last load just inside the door, King said, "I'll take the car down to the garage and help you with this stuff when I get back."

"Great!" Abbi said. "While you do that, I'll go put together a couple of sandwiches for lunch."

Sitting at the kitchen table a short while later, Abbi asked, "When do you plan to let your friend Megan know we are home? Please give me a few days before you ask her to visit. Maria and Squire have off until Wednesday, and I'd like to have some time for us to get the house at least dusted before we have company in."

"No problem. I need to go into town tomorrow for my meeting on that office building expansion for the bank, so let's ask Megan over for dinner on Friday night. Will that be O.K. with you?"

"Sure"

"Then I'll call her right after lunch to set it up. Oh, by the way, remind me to talk to Squire about replacing the light bulbs in the garage. When I was down there just now, I noticed several of them were out. I could do it myself, of course, but I need to let Squire think he is still useful. As you know, I really don't need a 'man of all jobs' anymore, but he has gotten to be a habit."

"Tell me again, exactly how long they have been working for you?"

"Since I finished building this house about eight years ago. Squire was working as a cowboy down at the ranch then, and Maria did laundry for some of the other guys and did most of the cooking after my mom got sick. He asked if he and Maria could come work for me. At the time I was putting in 16-hour days at work, trying to bring in enough money to pay for this place and build a reputation for my architectural firm, so I said yes. Maria took over as housekeeper and cook and Squire did any odd jobs that needed doing and took care of my horse. That is also about the same time he gave himself the nickname "Squire". As he said then, "Every King living in a castle needs a squire, so I'm it!"

Abbi chuckled at that and said, "Well, I am very glad to have Maria here. She is a big help with the twins, especially when I am facing a deadline for my costumes. Come to think of it, I have one coming up soon, so I had better get the kiddos down for a nap and get busy in the sewing room."

For several years, Abbi had been making costumes for the old-fashioned "showboat" tours that went up and down the Mississippi River, and for some of the museums along the way that dressed their guides in the pre-Civil War time period. She and Sam had even bought a mill that produced the special prints used for the dresses. Sam designed the small motifs used and Abbi made up some of the fabric into costumes. They were able to sell the extra fabric to craft stores and had built up a large list of clients.

"O.K." King said. "I'll help you get the twins down, then I'm going to spend some time in my office here working on a project I've been thinking about starting. It's an idea for something here at the house, but I'm not going to tell you yet. Let me get it all planned out, then I'll share."

"Oh, I do like surprises! Let's just put the dishes in the sink for now and I'll do them later, along with the ones from dinner."

Several hours later, the twins woke up and put a stop to Abbi's time in her sewing room. Putting them back into the playpen, she sat in her favorite chair and started sewing buttons on the dress she had almost finished. Pretty soon, the noisy beats on the toy drums, along with the giggles and squeals brought King out of his office. He immediately picked up a child in each arm and sat on the floor to play. Abbi put her sewing into the basket by her chair and joined them in the fun.

After Rona and Ren were in bed that night, King asked Abbi to join him at the dining room table. He spread out several sheets of drawing paper with plans already on them, plus a few blank pages. "This, my Love, is what I have been working on in my spare time for the last several months. I'd like to know what you think of it."

"Oh, goody! What am I looking at here?"

Taking a pencil to point out things, King said, "Well, this is our garage, and here, just on the other side of the cave wall, is where I would like to put this next project. It's an indoor – outdoor swimming pool!"

"A what?"

"Remember when we first discovered the tunnels and cave at Granny Edi's and Will started talking about putting in a swimming pool there?"

"Well, yes. I remember him talking about it, but what does that have to do with these plans?"

"It got me thinking about how great it would be to have a cooling swim out here in the almost dessert our range-land is. The horses don't mind the heat so much, but sometimes it gets really hot for us humans. I thought it would be nice, especially for you and the kids, if we had some way to cool off without having to stay inside with the air conditioner going full blast!"

"Wow!" Tell me more!"

"Well, here's my plan. We would need to leave as much of the cave wall as possible here on this side of the garage, since it is a major part of the foundation rock for the house, but we could cut a door right here next to the elevator. That would get us out to the small cave there. As you know, it has a short tunnel going up and into that larger cave with the outside opening just around the corner from the garage. Right now, Squire uses that area to store all the tools he needs to keep the outside of out tower cleaned up. Not much grass to cut, of course, but he does use that tractor and bush hog to keep the tumbleweeds and other range bushes from crowding right up to the base of the tower. Then he uses the rake to get them into a pile and burns them. I'm thinking that equipment could be moved to the smaller cave on the other side of the garage. You know, the one just to the right of the stable and hay storage caves. Squire could use the ramp we built for the horses to move the tractor in and out."

"O.K., once that is done, what's next? You said indoor – outdoor pool. What do you mean by that?"

"How would you like this idea? Say we build a paved patio and party area that covers almost the entire floor of the big cave. Then we build a large deck next to that patio that goes from the inside of the cave, down in levels almost to the ground, and wraps around that side of our tower for a gathering place? We could then build an above ground pool into that deck so that one end of it is inside the cave and the other end is outside. Depending on whether you wanted to swim or relax in the sun, or come into the cooler end, you could do either and not even get out of the pool. We could have our very own 'Summer Kitchen' almost like the one at Melrose Farm! Out here in Texas, the water would almost always be hot during the day, but I understand there is a system of sprayers that circulate a mist and cool it down to a comfortable temperature."

"Oh, King, this sounds wonderful! It would be a great place for our children to play in the fresh air without the danger of sunburn. I try to get them outside to play around the tower as often as possible, but it gets too hot very quickly, and the sand burns our feet. Would the inside part be big enough to put up a swing set? They are getting big enough now to enjoy it, but I couldn't think of where to put it"

"That is a huge cave, Love. We can make sure there is room for a play yard with enough equipment to keep them entertained for hours! Maybe even a kiddie pool just for them. It would be like having their own park!"

"Oooh! I can just see the birthday parties we can have for them!"

"Right! Not to mention all the parties for the adults! I really think this will be a great addition to our home."

"Yes! So, when can we get started?"

"I'll call my 'stonecutter' friend tomorrow and see when he can get his crew out to blow the door. While we are waiting for them, Squire and I can start moving the yard tools and equipment over to the other side. Then once the door is finished, I'd like to concentrate on turning the smaller cave into a dressing room and towel storage area. I really need to talk to Megan and see what her project is and how much time it will take. That will pretty much tell me when we can get this pool idea started."

"True. And speaking of time, we both have a busy day tomorrow, so I need to get to bed."

"Yeah, me too. You go ahead and I'll be along as soon as I get these plans back into my office."

Chapter Five

A S THE DINNER HOUR approached on Friday evening, Abbi did a quick look around her home to make sure everything was neat and dust free. This was the first time she had entertained one of King's childhood friends and she wanted to make sure the house made a good impression.

Maria had prepared one of her special dinners and was putting the finishing touches to the table just as King came out of his office. As he passed her on the way to the living room, she said, "You and Miss Megan have grown up much, Si? You will have no throwing of the food across the table as in the past, yes?"

King threw his head back and laughed. "Yes, we have grown beyond the throwing of the food, and will behave ourselves. This is business meeting, after all, between two businesspeople. Megan is coming for a serious talk, so there will be no time for playing around."

Just as Abbi finished changing Loren into a clean playsuit, the doorbell rang. King put Rona into the playpen and went to answer the door.

Megan walked in and gave him a big hug. "Oh, King, it is so good to see you after all these years! From what I see so far, I must say, what you have done with our old play tower is incredible! How in the world did you ever come up with the idea of turning this old pile of rocks into a home? Can I get a full tour? And driving up on your driveway sure beats that climb we used to take to get this high. You remember, Katie and I were never comfortable climbing the outside like you and Bob. Coming up through the tunnels was hard enough for us."

"Ah, Meggie, still the chatterbox, I see. Slow down and come meet Abbie and the twins, then we can talk."

Abbi had put Ren into the playpen with his sister and went to stand beside King. Extending her hand, she said, "Welcome to our home, Megan. From the stories I've heard, you guys had a fun-filled childhood. I just heard Marie say something about 'food fights?"

"Marie! Surely not 'Auntie Marie' of the wooden-spoon-across-the-knuckles Marie!"

"Yep, the same one. And you will get to see Carlos too. He went into town to mail some documents for me, but he should be back anytime. By the way, he now likes to be called 'Squire', as in 'Squire of the Castle'. Come on into the living room and we'll have a drink while we wait for dinner. Would you prefer wine or a soda?"

Megan sat down on the sofa, accepted her glass of wine from Abbi, and looked around.

"Oh, King! I am truly amazed! If I remember correctly, this was two small caves and that area you turned into the drive turnaround and small patio was just a wide ledge."

"Correct on all counts. I had to take advantage of where the ledge was located for the drive and front door, otherwise

I would have made the entrance higher up. But it all worked out, because I have put in staircases to the upper two stories, as well as a couple of floors down. There is a small balcony outside the Master bedroom, and we can see the Circle M from there. I'll show it to you later."

"So, you have turned this into a fairly large house! How many square feet?"

"I'd say about 4500 sq. feet, if you count the garage level."

"And you have how many bedrooms and baths? Abbi, I'm sorry if all my questions sound too personal, but building out an existing building is exactly why I need to talk with King, so my questions really fall into the business category. I hope you don't mind too much if I quiz you both on what you have here."

Just then, Marie came in to tell them dinner was ready. Megan jumped up and ran to give her a hug, which turned into a joint hug and squealing session.

"Now, Miss Megan, you just calm down and come eat dinner. I made your favorite enchiladas."

As they all took their seats and filled plates, Abbi said to Megan, "To answer your questions about the house, please feel free to ask anything you like. I love to brag about my husband's work. But first, answer a couple of questions for me, please. What made you call King? I thought you two had not talked to each other in years. How did you know he could help you?"

Megan turned to King and said, "Abbi has not met my mother yet, has she?" Turning back to Abbi, she said, "My Mother is well known for her scrapbooking. She collects news clippings and gossip from all the neighbors and puts it all into albums. She has a big spread on what King, and someone named Russell Mayhew did with an old hotel. After reading that, I knew he was just the person I needed to talk too.

King said, "Well, just to help you catch up on the news, and so your mom can add to her scrapbook, that 'someone named Russell' is not only the other half of Mayhew - Cole Construction, but he is also Katie's husband. They just adopted an infant girl named Susan. Now that you are home from wherever you have been these last few years, I'll ask them to pay a visit so you and Katie can catch up."

"Well, you see, where I've been is one of the reasons I'm here. I have spent the last four years in Paris, learning how to be a Cordon Blue Chief. King, do you remember my Uncle Travis? He visited the Circle M several times when we were children."

"Yea, big tough-looking guy, but with a big smile. He always intimidated me a bit."

"Mother's brother does look intimidating, but he has a heart of gold. He has made a fortune in the oil business and is now into politics. He never married, so has no heirs, and has recently declared my two brothers and me his heirs."

"Wow! Set to inherit scads of oil money! You must be thrilled."

"Wait! The inheritance comes with caveats. He says quote. "You must prove yourselves worthy of handling it responsibility" unquote. He has given my two brothers an oil well each. They must show a substantial profit by the end of the year to prove themselves and earn the deed from him. However, he also says that the boys will only have to take one or two steps to be able to handle the job, but because I am a female, I will have to take one hundred and one steps to prove myself. He is not really someone that thinks less of women, he just knows how the business world works. Because of my cooking career, he knew I would not want an oil well, so he has given me an old building."

Abbi almost shouted, "A building! How can you prove yourself with an old building?"

Megan smiled and said "That is exactly why I need King's help! You see, this building is actually two separate, very narrow buildings, side by side, in one of the most run-down sections of 'THE BIG CITY' as Uncle Travis calls it, but it is still fairly close to downtown. This area is just beginning to reinvent itself, with new owners and new business moving in, but this building has been abandoned for almost two decades. It is in terrible shape right now, but I hope King can help me re-build the inside and turn it into a Five Star Restaurant. There is great potential for the whole area, and I'd like to be a part of that. Will you help me, King?"

"King?"

"King? Did you hear me?"

"What? Oh, yes, I heard you. Ah, Meggie, you caught me by surprise. Of course, I'll help you. I just never thought your project would turn out to something on this scale. I was just thinking about what would be needed first. I think the first thing would be to a drive up there to look it over. That will help me figure out what needs to be done."

"Yes! I already have the key, so we can go up anytime. Abbi, you, and the twins come too. We can make a round trip in one day, so it would be an adventure. Oh, King, thank you! If I can make this work, it will not only prove to my Uncle

I can handle money responsibility, but it will also prove to myself I can run a great Restaurant. And speaking of money, now that you have agreed to work with me, I can tell you. As part of the deal for having to take 'one hundred and one steps' instead of just a few like my brothers, Uncle Travis said that if I could convince you to do this, he will give me not only your fee, but also half the renovation costs as the bills come due. He says that will count as the first step!"

"He trusts me that much?"

"Oh, yes. Mama has kept him up to date over the years, so he knows your history with unusual projects. He will want to see the plans before he commits to anything, but I'm sure he will like whatever you come up with.

Chapter Six

THE DRIVE UP FOUR days later proved to be fun. Abbi and Megan formed a close friendship along the way, and King joined in the conversations by reminiscing over things about his and Megan's childhood. Toward the end of the trip, Abbi was comfortable enough to share some of her early life, and even touched on how she became familiar with the people at Melrose Farm.

Slowing down to almost a crawl as they neared Megan's building, King looked closely at the surrounding area. He told the ladies he wanted to get a feel of the neighborhood, so he could better fit her new restaurant into the street scene.

"Not too modern on the outside, I would think. It looks as if the overall re-do of the neighborhood is to keep the Traditional look for the outside and keep the new ideas for the inside. That works for me! We did that with the hotel we turned into a retirement home. Meggie, where is a good place to park?"

"Turn left at the next corner and go to the alley. There is a small parking area just behind the buildings. Abbi, since I'm not sure how safe this old heap is, you may not want to take the babies inside. Feel free to peek in when I get the door open, but if you don't like what you see, you can go beyond the alley and keep on down that street about two blocks. There is a tiny park where the twins could run around. King and I can meet you there when we finish looking around."

"Thanks for the warning! I'll just grab a quick look inside so I will know what King is getting himself into. After that I would just be in the way, so the kids and I will go to the park. Marie packed a huge lunch for us, so I'll take that along as I go. King, could you please put the basket in the bottom of the stroller?"

As Megan began unlocking the backdoor, she told them both to stand back several steps for a minute or two. She opened the door and let it crash hard against the side of the building, then picked up a baseball bat that was leaning against the door frame right inside. She stepped in, whacked the bat against the wall a couple of times, the sound echoing through the empty building. She backed out quickly and moved to stand just in front of Abbi and the twins, raising her arms out to the sides as if to guard the stroller. Suddenly, there was a whirring sound, followed by a very large flock of pigeons escaping out the door. Others were seen flying out of two broken windows at the top of the building.

"These guys will have to find a new home, but I haven't called the exterminators yet. I wanted to see if I had a chance of taking over here before I displaced them."

"O.K. Well, that tells me the first thing to do is seal up any broken windows so they can't get back in!" King got busy jotting notes in the book in his hand. "An exterminator is a good idea, though. You probably have more than pigeons living in here. Rats, mice, maybe even larger animals. If this place has been vacant and closed for decades, anything may have made it their home. You don't know if any vagrants have moved in, do you?"

"When Uncle Travis and I came to look a couple of months ago, we did not see any signs that someone had been living here. Actually, the man that owns the antique shop three doors down the street told us that the homeless will not go in because it is haunted!"

"Haunted!" Abbi said. "Who believes in that stuff anymore?"

"I'm not sure, but I do know there are some weird noises in here. We will probably find out where they are coming from as we renovate. Uncle Travis said that haunted story is why it has been empty for so long and the reason he could buy it so cheaply."

"Hey! This just keeps getting better and better!" King said. "Let's go take a look."

As they stepped through the door, Megan hit a switch and flooded an area of about six by eight feet with light. At least enough to see they were in a small room with an open door straight ahead and stairs going down to the basement on one side.

"Sorry, but from now on, we will need the flashlights I brought. Uncle Travis had some of his guys bring in a small generator and enough lights for this room, but nothing else. We were afraid to have the city turn on the electricity to the building because the wiring is so old."

Abbi went over to the door and put just her head through. Aiming the flashlight Megan had given her around, she said, "Oh, my God! Sorry, but this is just too scary. I'm going to leave now. See you at the park!" She hurriedly pushed the stroller through the outside door and almost ran across the parking lot.

"What have you got here, Meggie? Let me see what is so scary!" King went over to the open door and took a step inside. Flashing his light around, he said, "Woah! I can see what she means! This does remind me of that hotel when Russell and I first explored it. You haven't had any fires here like the hotel, but time itself has caused a lot of damage."

"Yes, I told you it was a disaster. Uncle Travis always liked to give us challenges.

As they walked further into the building, more damage became evident. He and Megan spent a good two hours going over the space, King constantly taking notes. Finally deciding they could do no more, they left to meet Abbi at the park. She had taken over one of the tables, spread out some of the snacks from the basket, and was happily sewing on buttons while the twins took a nap on a quilt under the oak tree.

She asked, "So, did you declare it a lost cause? Or can it be saved?"

King laughed, then said, "Megan was right when she told us it is a disaster, but with hard work, time, and lots of money, it can be saved. You had better be glad your uncle is picking up the tab for half of it, Megan."

"Believe me, I knew that after the first time I saw the place."

King said to Abbi, "I'm glad you didn't take the babies in, Love. Not only is it dark in there, but it also smells bad from the lack of fresh air getting in, and it is dangerous. Some of the floors have rotted through, and beams are hanging down all over the place. Your Uncle has really given you a challenge this time, Meggie. It's going to be a huge one even getting to the point we can start rebuilding."

Abbi handed each of them a wet cloth she had taken out of a plastic bag. "Here, wash your hands and eat while you tell me the rest."

Once they all had a plate piled with lunch, King said, "Meggie, I think the best thing to do if we want this project to be done correctly, is to gut the entire space out to the exterior walls, top to bottom, including the basement. That way, we will have a clean slate to work with. The exterior walls seem to be in good shape, so there shouldn't be any problems there. While I am drawing up some preliminary plans, I'd like you do three things."

As he ticked them off on his fingers, he said, "1. Get the exterminators out here and ask them to give it a through treatment, inside and out, including spraying for ants and termites in the basement. 2. Call the utility companies and get a large water line and heavy-duty electric lines run. Also, sewer lines. We can extend all of them into the building when we are ready to pull out the old ones and replace them with new. Since you are on a corner lot, it should not cost too much for them to bring the services in from the street. Have them run everything up close to the back door on the end unit. You'll need to figure out how much water pressure and power you will need for a fully functioning restaurant. No need to have them come out twice to upgrade if you can have that information at the start. And 3. Get a large trash collection container put in your parking area. There's going to be a lot of junk coming out of the building and we need somewhere to dump it."

"Sure, I'll get on those things right away. You really want me to get involved with this part of the process?"

"Of course! It is going to be your restaurant, so you should be a part of re-doing the space. That way, you won't be mad at me at the end if it isn't exactly what you wanted. Russell and I have found that by involving our clients from the beginning, it's better for everyone. Problems can get fixed before they become overwhelming, and the client seems happier with the whole job. Besides, since you are the owner of the property, it will be much easier for you to get the job done with less paperwork.

"That sounds reasonable. I had just assumed you knew better than me what had to be done, so I would just stay out of the way and let you do it. But I'll love being a part of making it work! Thank you!"

"You'll have to thank Russell for that one. He is the one that convinced me it is the best way to go. And while we are talking about Russell, would you mind if I call him in on this? He is much better at interior spaces than I am. I have no problem with the big picture, but he is a whiz at making use of all the interior spaces and doing it is such a way it looks marvelous when he finishes. If you want this to be an up-scale dining establishment, I think we need his input."

"Of course, call him in. I had already thought you would do that anyway. You are partners after all. If he comes out here to 'consult', please tell him to bring Katie and their baby. You said her name is Susan?"

"Yes. Susan was already her name and Katie added Elizabeth to honor the nurse that helped them so much with the adoption. Now that Katie knows you are home, it wouldn't surprise me if they are already making plans to come."

Abbi had finished eating while the other two talked, so began clearing up the picnic things, and repacking the basket. As she was doing this, she asked Megan, "King told me you are living with your parents at your ranch. I know we made this trip in only a couple of hours today, but isn't living there and having your restaurant here going to be a rather long commute?"

"Ah, Abbi, I'm glad you reminded me. King, that is something I wanted to ask you. Now that you have seen the space, do you think you could plan in a small apartment for me? It would not have to be much. Just enough to let me live in it until I can get the restaurant up and running. Then I could turn it over to a manager and get a larger place."

"We can do that. From what I've seen today, we may have to think hard to find ways to use all the space you'll have!"

Abbi said, "What do you mean, King?"

"Well, it looks like two structures with a common wall between them. But from what I could see today, it looks as if the building was built as only one unit and that center wall added later. Making a quick study today, I think we can tear out that wall completely to open up the space. The whole thing is three stories tall with a full basement under all of it. That's a lot of square feet, Megan. There should be no problem at all putting in an apartment for you."

"Oh, this is getting so exciting! I can't wait to tell Uncle Travis he didn't buy two buildings, but only one! He is gonna' flip!"

The twins were waking up, so they finished clearing up the picnic things, and soon headed back to the car. On the way home, they decided to get together at the Castle in a few days to go over plans. King asked Megan to write up a list of questions or requirements for what she wanted, and he would get in touch with Russell to see when the Mayhews' could come to Texas.

Chapter Seven

LATER THAT EVENING, KING came out of his home office laughing. When he joined Abbi in the living room, she asked him what was so funny.

"It's just that I know my sister so well! I just called Russell to tell him about Megan's project and find out if he could help with it. He said he has one more job of his own to finish up tomorrow and they will be on the way here the day after! Katie is already packed. Russell said she hasn't stopped talking about getting out here as soon as possible since she talked to Megan last week."

"That's great that they are coming! How long do you think they will be able to stay? I'm guessing Katie and Megan will have a lot to catch up on. It sounds like they were very close growing up."

"Practically joined at the hip as the saying goes. As a matter of fact, all members of both families were very close. The kids sort of drifted apart as they got older and had more responsibilities and jobs to do on the ranches, but we all continued to visit back and forth often. I should probably call James and Johnny and get together again."

"Will you go to pick them up in the corporate plane, or are they flying commercially?"

"Neither! They are driving out! Russell said Katie wants to have a car available while she is here, and they are due for a vacation anyway. They are planning to be here at least two weeks. Katie said they can stay in her old room at the ranch with Bob and Ruth if that would work better for you."

"Nonsense! I will love having them here. Megan will be meeting with you and Russell, so Katie should be around then also. She and Megan can grab 'talk time' between your work sessions."

"Super! You know what? If they are driving, it will take them at least three days. That will give my stone blasting guys time to get the new door put in. Then Squire and I can move the outdoor tools and clean out the big cave. With the addition of some lawn furniture, you ladies can have a nice place to gather out of the sun."

"Oh, wonderful! You know, I have been thinking about that project and have some ideas if you would care to hear them."

"Sure. What do you have in mind?"

"Well, your talking about Bob and Ruth reminded me of something I've wanted to ask you for a long time. Did you know I'm a bit jealous of them? Well, not them exactly, but their yard."

"Their yard! What do you mean?"

"The lovely green grass and the wonderful trees. I was wondering how hard it would be to actually start a real lawn around our tower."

"What? You don't like the sand and sagebrush and cactus? Kidding! It would just take time and a lot of water, but we can certainly get started on it right away. Being a guy, I never gave it much thought, but having real grass and a few trees around would make this place more attractive. As soon as we get the cave cleaned out, I'll have Squire start cutting the range land back and then we can lay out the boundary of your lawn."

"Really? Oh, you are so good to me! So different from that creep I was married to before."

"Hey, I thought you were not going to think about that jerk anymore. Now, all you should think about is how much I love you, and nothing else about that time with him. O.K.?"

"Yes, you're right. Fine then. If you love me so much, how would you like to help me get the twins down for the night?"

"Not fair! But I'll help. You know I like doing that anyway."

By the time the Mayhews' pulled into the driveway four days later, the door was in, the cave cleaned out, lawn chairs, tables, and some play equipment scattered around, and Squire had a wide swath of ground cleared around the base of the tower. After being told of the overall plans for the new yard, deck and swimming pool, Russell and King quickly measured lines and drove stakes for the yard boundaries and deck foundations. Then Megan came over and all thoughts of improving "King's Castle" were put on hold.

At least for the three most concerned with the new restaurant. Abbi and Katie took the twins down to their new play yard. They sat at one of the tables and talked about Abbi's plans for the new lawn while the twins enjoyed the fresh air and their new swing set. Susan was still a bit too young to be on the swings, but she enjoyed crawling around on the big quilt her mother put down for her. Maria brought down cool drinks and stayed to chat awhile, then Squire could be seen spreading grass seed on the bare ground outside the cave. Maria took him a glass of lemonade, then gathered all the snack bowls and empty glasses and went back upstairs.

Megan and the two gentlemen settled around the dinning room table and got down to serious plans. Megan liked Russell right away and told him so.

"Well, then. That will make this whole project go better. It's always easier to work with a client that likes me!"

After a chuckle, King said, "O.K., Meggie, do you have that list of questions I asked you to write up?"

"Yes, I do. But before we tackle those questions, I want to let you know about all those tasks you put on my shoulders. The electricity wires have already been brought across the street and connected to a breaker right at the corner of the building. Extra heavy-duty to cover the kitchen equipment once it goes in. The water and sewer pipes are scheduled to go in next week, and the trash container can be delivered whenever we start tearing out the old wood. They said there was no need to pay the rental fee until it was needed. The exterminator was out there yesterday and sprayed the entire building on the inside and all along the outside at ground level. His people even went up on ladders and covered the broken windows with cardboard to keep the pigeons out. So, there! I CAN be of use!"

King said, "Your Uncle Travis would be proud of you! And I am too. Getting these things done will really help us get started on the job of redoing the inside. Thanks."

Russell added, "It sounds like you are committed to making this a reality. My hat is off to you. Now, about those questions and any 'wishes' you might have about your restaurant. Anything special we need to plan for?"

"As for anything special, I guess only the small apartment I talked to King about. I really would like to have a Five Star Restaurant specializing in organic food as much as possible, and with a clean, uncluttered but comfortable atmosphere. I would like my customers to feel they could just walk in off the street in blue jeans or dress up for an evening out and be comfortable either way. Can you guys come up with a design like that?"

King said, "I think we can do that. Right now, though, we need to get Russell up there so he can see exactly what we must work with. Could you go up with us tomorrow?"

"Sure. Let's leave early, though. I need to get back in time to have a conference call with a couple of fellows I hope to hire to help with the restaurant cooking."

"O.K. Suppose I pick you up at the Circle M about eight tomorrow morning."

"Great! Now, would you care to show me this in-home elevator I've heard about? You showed the upstairs doors to me the last time I was here, but we didn't go down. Why an elevator anyway?"

"Don't you remember that climb through all the tunnels when we were kids? I knew I did not want to do that to get into my own home, so an elevator was the next best thing. Come on! I know Katie wants to bend your ear for a couple of hours, anyway. Let's go join them."

The Mayhews and Coles were just settling in the living room to enjoy their after-dinner drinks when Katie asked King, "So, you are abducting my husband tomorrow, huh?"

"Yep, early in the morning. Very early. I need to run by my office in town before we head up to see Megan's building. If Russell is to get a good idea of what we must deal with, he is going to need more light than those small flashlights we had the last time. I want to pick up several of those large units we use for construction sites. We can just leave them there, since we will need them until we get the electric wires brought into the building. What do you ladies have planned?"

Katie replied, "I'm taking Susan down to the ranch to visit with Ruth and Bob, and their baby. It's hard to believe Evan is the same age as your twins, and I haven't seen him since Susan's Christening party. Are you planning to come with me, Abbi?"

"Yes, I am. I want to talk to Ruth about what flowers she has planted around the house. I realized they can't be the same ones you and Sam have at Melrose Farm, but I want to know which ones will do well in the heat we have here. I just can't wait to get started on our project for the deck and yard downstairs!"

King told her, "Well, plan out what you want on paper, but I'm afraid the rest of it will have to wait for a while. Russell and I will be tied up with Megan's restaurant for the next few weeks. Oh, I'm sure there will be some "down time" when we have to wait for something to happen, so I can get people out here to work on it, but it will be a slow process."

Russell spoke up to say, "King, I think both your Abbi and my Katie have learned the construction business well enough to know our work has to come before any home projects. But I also know my Katie gets very 'antsy' while she waits for those home projects to get started. Plus, if I remember correctly, you had this place pretty much finished before you got married and even the addition of her sewing room was pretty much your project before she moved here. It's only natural that Abbi wants to start this new project quickly. It will be her first venture into a joint home project with you."

"Oh, Russell, thank you! That's exactly how I feel! King, I understand Megan's project comes first! But I just like thinking about how I would like to have things done with the pool and the deck and the yard. Just think, maybe I can even have a small vegetable garden!"

Chapter Eight

ONCE THE MAYHEW – COLE Construction team and Megan arrived at her building, Russell took the time to walk around and examine the outside of the building. He and King checked for loose bricks, shook drainpipes to see if they were attached properly, and checked to see if water was being funneled away from the building properly. He told Megan, "We will have to put up scaffolding on the sidewalk to check out the upper floors. Can you contact the city to see what permits we need for that? You could even go ahead and apply for them. King told me you wanted to be involved, so I'm taking advantage of your interest."

"Great! Yes, the more I have a hand in the renovations, the more I will feel like it's really mine. Ask me to do anything but swing a hammer!"

Both men laughed at that, then King said, "O.K. Russell, ready to go inside?"

Megan opened the back door and they all stepped into the small room. Switching on two of the large lights, Russell and King moved forward, with Megan bringing up the rear with her small flashlight. Carefully avoiding the holes where the floor had rotted out, they moved toward the front of the building.

Russell said, "Being on the outside lot will give us more options for the interior, and I really like the way the corner of the building was recessed and used for the doorway. That will be a great focal point for your new entrance. King, you said this may have been one space when it was first built? If we find that to be true, maybe we should consider taking out the other front door and replacing it with a large window."

Cautiously moving around the building, they covered the whole area a lot faster than on the first trip. Having enough light to see more than three feet ahead of them allowed for faster movement.

King said, "I now see this top floor has a ceiling. Megan, what is in the attic?"

"You know, I can't really say. Uncle Travis and I never went up there."

"Well, that is something we can explore another day. It is beginning to get too hot in here. I say we leave the rest for another time. Russell and I can get started on drawing up some preliminary plans. I wish we had Melissa here to take some "before" pictures for us. They might even help us plan the "after" results."

Russell said, "You know, Meli and Will just might be able to come out here for a couple of days. Will has some time off from the college for Spring Break and with Maggie to care for, Meli hasn't started on her new photography book yet. They might enjoy a short trip. Can you and Abbi put up with another baby in the house?"

"Of course! I'll call Meli right now." Looking at his phone, he added, "Well, at least as soon as we get outside. Megan, something to add to your list of things to do. Get someone to come give you an estimate on putting Wi-Fi and cell phone service in here."

"O.K. Umm, I think I remember you talking about Will, but who are Melissa and Maggie?"

King answered her by saying, "Will's wife and new daughter. Did your mom-who-knows-all-the-gossip happen to write to you about the "mystery guest" I had at the Castle some time ago?" At her nod in the affirmative, he continued. "Well, Meli was that mystery guest. She is also a photo/journalist, so loves to take pictures of everything. I'm sure she would love to add this to her list of adventures."

"Oh, my mother would love that!" Megan said. "She could make up a scrapbook for me. Hey! Even better! Meli publishes books of her photographs? Do you think she would do one for me? It would be a wonderful advertisement and souvenir for the restaurant, and to have on display at the front desk. I'd be happy to pay her"

"I'll ask as soon as I get a signal."

They went back to the small room just inside the back door, left the large lights on the floor, and went out into the parking lot. As King stepped away and started dialing his phone, Russell and Megan discussed what needed to be done to the space dedicated to parking cars.

Russell said, "Even with the double wide building, by the time you get your permanent trash bin and all the services needed for your restaurant, and room for deliveries, this will not be big enough for more than four or five cars. What about your customers? Is there street parking allowed. What about a public parking lot or multiple level garage?"

"That was one of the things that swayed Uncle Travis to buy here. He knew the city is trying to help the remodeling of this area and they have already planned to build a large parking garage two blocks away. No street parking, though, except on the side streets. The main street out front will be turned into a 'Walking Mall' with no vehicles allowed. They are even going to remove the high curbs, so everything flows crossing back and forth from one side of the street to the other. They are hoping to turn this ten-block area into a 'Travel Destination for Shopping' while tourists are visiting our city. The shop owners that I have talked to also want to attract locals for a constant source of customers."

"Hey! That could turn into a big plus for your restaurant! Build up a good appetite getting to it, then walk off some of the calories while shopping or getting back to your car. Win, win!"

"Ha! You're funny. But I do see your point."

"It looks like King is still talking to either Will or Meli. Let's get in the car and turn on the air conditioning. Is it usually this hot so early in the year?"

"Russell, Texas is hot all year! Well, further north, they do have 'Winters'. Even with snow sometimes, but this far south, it is usually pretty warm most of the year."

Chapter Nine

"Yo! Megan! Meli jumped at the chance to put together a book for you! She said that with this one, she knew she would have Katie and Abbi to look after Maddie while she took pictures. Will was there and said as soon as they can get packed and make sure Sam is available to take care of Granny Edi, they could head this way. He only has a few more days off though, then his teaching job starts up again. Russell, I think it might be best if I take the jet and go pick them up. That way, Meli will have more time to get her 'before' pictures, and there would be no problem with us getting started on the building sooner. If I leave early tomorrow morning, have Sam bring them to the airport to meet me, we can do a quick gas up and turn around. We should be able to be back here for dinner tomorrow night. Want to join us, Megan?"

"Well, sure, but how is Abbie going to deal with all of these changes to her life? I mean, two extra people plus a baby as guests for several days, and a dinner party to plan on such short notice. Come on, that's a lot to ask."

King and Russell both threw back their heads and laughed. When King had his breath back, he said, "You haven't known my Abbi long enough to understand how wonderful she is. Or how this whole extended family goes the extra mile for each other. Until Abbi got involved with them and then married me, she hadn't had that closeness for a very long time. She was always close to her half-brother Jeff, of course, but he was living his own life and they seldom saw each other. Now she thrives on having all this 'family time' and loves every minute of it. Come on, let's head home, and I'll call her on the way to give her a heads up on the new plans."

While the building inspection had been going on, Abbi and her twins, Katie and her Susan, and Ruth with her son Evan were enjoying a visit sitting in a grouping of lawn chairs in Ruth's yard. Bob was out by the barn helping clean tack, so the ladies were having a 'girl talk' about a variety of subjects.

After Katie and Ruth finished catching up on gossip of the family, Abbi turned to Ruth and said, "I know King has told you and Bob about the new project we want to do up at the castle, but could you answer a few questions for me, please? I just love your shady yard and all the green grass and would like to have the same things up at our home. What kinds of grass and flowers do you find grow best here?"

Ruth chuckled and said, "Not much of anything! Kidding, almost. To seriously answer your question, you must realize that most of what you see was here long before I came along. Katie, it was your great-grandparents that established this ranch, right?"

"Yes, and I remember my grandfather talking about how barren the yard was when he was a child. His mother planted this tree we are sitting under the first year they were here. She kept it watered every day with water from the creek. She would go down with a bucket and haul it up here by herself because the men were too busy trying to establish the ranch. They couldn't be bothered with something as silly as watering a tree. Of course, when her children got big enough, she turned that job over to them. Later, Grammy Cole added other trees and planted the roses over there, but all of it had to be hand-watered every day. I am so glad that my Granddaddy was able to build the sprinkler system fed by the new water tower. That made the yard so much easier to keep up with and allowed him to plant grass seeds. Before that, the yard was just mostly hard-packed dirt and weeds."

Ruth said, "So, you see, Katie, I didn't have a lot to do with this yard. It was already well established when I married Bob. I have added a few flower beds here and there, and I'll help you get some of your own going once your new yard is ready. But if you want shade trees and flower beds, you need to tell King to plan a watering system right at the very beginning. Trees grow very slowly, you know, so you will need to buy the most mature ones you can find and make sure they have lots of water. A good plant food in the first few years would help, too."

Katie added, "Something you can do right now, Abbi, is start a compost pile. Have Marie save all the vegetable scraps when she cooks, and pile them in a special place. The stuff will have to be turned often so it rots evenly, but it will help your trees and flowers grow much better. They can't get much nourishment from this range dirt that is mostly sand."

"Yes, indeed." Ruth added. "Remind me to show you my compost pile and how to take care of it. Now, there is something else I want to talk to you about. Katie, you will be interested in this too."

"Oh. What is that?"

"Well, you know I give riding lessons to children. One day last month, I had a call from a couple who had purchased a Companion Dog from Katie's Kennels back when you were living here. Their son remembered seeing me working with the horses and other children when they came out to pick up their dog and has been bugging his parents ever since. They finally called to see if I could teach their son how to ride a horse! Abbi, I was wondering if you might have some time to help me with that? I'm not sure it's something I want to tackle by myself, so I would like to have another adult here to steady the child while they are in the saddle. I've searched out the special saddles and other equipment I'll need, but I haven't ordered anything yet. I was waiting to see if you could help."

"Oh, that does sound like a daunting task, and something I'd really like to help with. Let me think about it for a while, will you? I'll have to check with Marie and see if she could watch the twins while I'm here. How much time do you think it would take for each lesson?"

"I'm not quite sure yet. They would have to be private lessons because I couldn't deal with more than one physically challenged child at the time. I'm thinking that I would have to tack up the horse myself instead of having the students do it as a part of their lesson. I can have the horse ready when each student arrives. That will cut the time needed for each lesson considerably, so maybe allow half an hour for each lesson?"

"O.K. I'll talk to Marie when I get home. When would you want to start?"

"Now that I know you will help, I'll go ahead and order a couple of the special saddles, and maybe even the lift. Once they get here, we could begin any time. Maybe we can even talk to Sadie Jenkins and see if she would be willing to watch all three babies while we give the lesson. I have been using her as an occasional sitter for Evan ever since he was born, and she is great. I'll also need to talk to Bob about which horse…"

Bob had come up behind his wife and now broke in to ask, "Ask me what, Ruthie?"

"Oh! You startled me! Ask you which of our horses would be best for those special riding lessons I talked to you about last week. Abbi would like to help, so we can do this now."

"Right! But can we talk about that later? Now we need to greet these people driving up the lane."

They all turned to watch as King's car came closer. He pulled up close, so the car was in the shade, then got out and scooped Rona up to give her a smacking kiss. Ren was sleeping on the quilt, so King didn't bother him. Russell did the same with Susan, then the guys settled on the grass next to their wives.

King said to Abbi, "I have invited an extra for dinner tomorrow night. I already gave Marie a heads up, so I hope that is O.K. with you."

"Sure. Megan again?"

"Yep. Also, I'm going to do a quick trip back East tomorrow. Meli is going to do a book for the restaurant, so we need to get her out here for the "before" pictures as soon as possible"

Katie spoke up "Ummm, King? Since you are bringing Meli here, I think I should go back to help Sam. Could Susan and I go with you? Russell can stay here as long as needed, but I hate to think of all pressure on Sam's shoulders of seeing to Grannie Edi's needs plus the care of Katie's Kennel and overseeing Jude and the horses. Jeff tries to lend a hand, but he is usually so busy at the hospital he's not much help."

Russell said, "I'll really miss you and Susan, Love, but you are right. Sam is going to need some help with all of that."

"Well, if I'm to be ready to leave with you early in the morning, I need to get back and pack. Ruth, it was so good to see you and Bob again. You need to plan a trip to visit us, you know. Come anytime."

"We will, when Bob can take time off from the ranch."

"Yeah, like that's gonna' happen anytime soon!" Katie said as she picked up Susan. "Ah, Susie, I should have moved you sooner! Poor Baby, you've got the sun in your eyes."

King said, "Umm, Sis? Talking about the sun in her eyes makes me re-think our departure time. Can you possibly be packed and ready to leave within the hour? If we wait until tomorrow morning, I'm going to have the sun in my eyes both ways. Leaving now, we can be there around nine tonight, catch a couple of hours of sleep, then leave early in the morning to come back here."

"Sure. That makes a lot of sense. I don't need to pack much, and Russell can bring the rest whenever he heads back. Let's get back to the Castle!"

"Tell you what." King said. "You guys go back there and get packed, then Russell can bring you out to the airport. I'll go straight there from here and start getting the plane ready. That should cut about forty-five minutes off our departure time."

"O.K.! We'll see you there soon." Katie was busy grabbing all of Susan's toys and putting them into the huge diaper bag, then turned to her other brother.

"Good-buy, Bob. It was so nice to see you again. You, too, Ruth. Please come see us soon."

After quick hugs all around they piled into the car and headed back to the Castle. While Katie packed only what would be needed for her trip home, Abbie tossed a few things into a small bag for King.

As she handed it to Russell to put in the car, she said, "Since King leaves some things in our apartment there, he doesn't need to take a lot with him. You know, I thought the idea of building a complete apartment for us in your home was a waste of time and money, but we sure have used it a lot. Thank you for thinking of us!"

"Hey, Sis, that's what big brothers do! What are you giving me for supper tonight?"

"Whatever Maria has already fixed while I was visiting with Ruth! I'll make sure she has it on the table when you get back from the airport.

Chapter Ten

KATIE AND RUSSELL TALKED about the project for Megan all the way out to the airport. "I'm really getting excited about it!" Russell told her. "This is going to be even bigger than fixing up the old hotel, in terms of problems to solve and where to put things, and how to turn that big hollow space into a Five Star Restaurant. As soon as Melissa gets here and takes her "Before" pictures, we can really make some progress. Once all the rotten floors and rubble have been removed, we are going to start in the basement with the buildout of two apartments, one for Megan and one for either her new cook or a General Manager. Then we will work on the upper floors, but King and I still don't have all those drawing completed yet."

"Megan wants this to be more than just a restaurant, correct? I heard her mention a Ballroom and even a performance room for live entertainment."

"Yes, she will be in the perfect place for that. Her building is right in the middle of a new pedestrian mall, with upscale shops and two nice hotel chains that will be just blocks away."

"It does sound exciting! Maybe we can come back for the Grand Opening!"

"We can plan to do that! But right now, it looks as if King is ready to go. He will just have to wait while I give my Susan a hug and bunches of kisses. Her Mother, too! Bye, love. Meli and I will probably be back East as soon as she gets all the pictures she needs. All the rebuilding plans should be finished by then, and King won't need me here after that."

Katie pulled Susan and her car seat from the back of the car and hurried to strap them into the plane idling on the runway. King came over to the car and grabbed suitcases and bundles of things he was told just had to go home with Susan. He left Russell to bring the rest. As soon as he had stowed the luggage and made sure both Susan and Katie were buckled in, he started taxiing down the runway. Russell watched them until they were just a dot, then headed back toward King's Castle.

King had called ahead to talk about the change of plans, so Will met them at the airport.

"I came instead of Jeff. He had an emergency at the hospital, so was not going to get here before ten or so. I figured you would rather take your chances with me rather than sitting here waiting that long."

"Hey, you're not such a bad driver!" King said. "Certainly not as reckless as Sam! Scares me spitless every time I get into a car when she's driving!"

"You guys are just being mean! She really isn't that bad. Will, are you planning to go out with Meli tomorrow?"

"Yea, I thought I might. I do have those days off from the University, so the trip out there will be a nice change. Of course, I know Meli will have me carrying around her cameras, but that's O.K. Come on, Granny has some of her Peach Pie waiting for you."

The aroma of freshly brewed coffee met then at the door to the family room, and Sam was just coming in from the kitchen with a tray full of plates with pie. Meli followed with the coffee. They all settled in to enjoy the treat and to catch up on family news. They had been talking for about an hour when King stood and carried his empty cup and plate over to the tray. As he put them down, he said, "I need to leave early in the morning, Meli. Are you and Will all packed and ready to go?"

"Yep! Good to go right after an early breakfast. I just need to pack a few last-minute things for Maddie. Jeff is taking us to the airport on his way to the hospital."

"Great! Then I'll say goodnight to all of you and hit the sack."

Katie got up and said, "I'm right behind you. The sheets are freshly washed in your apartment, Bro. Thanks for bringing Susan and me home early. Don't leave in the morning until I get to hug you again!"

Just as she was about to go through the connecting door to the barn turned home and office, Sam called to her.

"Katie, that State Policeman that bought several of your pups stopped by while you were gone. He wanted to let you know he was planning to take two of them when he went out to the annual State Police Conference later this Summer. He will use them to give demonstrations to the new recruits. You can never guess where that Conference is going to be held! Right in the same city where your hubby and King are fixing up the restaurant! Is there a chance it might be finished by then?"

"Well, depending on exactly when the Conference will be held, it's possible. I'll call him tomorrow to find out the dates. Then King will know how fast he has to work!"

Chapter Eleven

THE FLIGHT BACK WAS uneventful. King landed the jet, taxied directly into his hanger, and stopped right next to his car he had parked inside the night before. The luggage and Meli's cameras were quickly transferred, and they headed out to The Castle. They had just stepped inside the front door when Maria came running from the kitchen. "My Nickki! Oh, it is so good to see you again!"

Using the name they had given Meli when they didn't know her real one, she gave a big hug, then stood back and asked, "Is this Gringo treating you well? Do I need to put Jalapenos in his cereal?"

"Oh, Maria, he treats me very well. I want to thank you again for treating me so well when I didn't even know who I was! But all of that is behind me now, and I can do what I was trained for. Take pictures! King tells me it is going to be a two-part job, so we will see each other often over the next few months."

"Bien, Bien! It is too early here for lunch, but I have some snacks ready. Go to your old room and unpack, then you will come relax in the living room, Si? You can put that beautiful baby right here in the playpen. My other two babies are still taking their morning nap, so she can get used to it on her own for now."

Abbi just shook her head when her Housekeeper, Cook, Nannie, friend took over as hostess and just followed Meli and Will into the bedroom.

"How many days do you have, Will?

"Only a long weekend, Abbi. I need to be back at the University by Tuesday. Classes begin on Wednesday, and I still have to finish preparing my first lecture."

"Well, that should not be a problem for you! As you are such a great archeologist, talking about it should be an easy thing for you. How do you like teaching at the University?"

"It's great! I may want to go on another 'dig' at some point, but only as an instructor during Summer Break."

"That sounds reasonable. Are you ready to go follow Maria's instructions, Meli?"

"Well, she did boss me around while I was a houseguest here. I guess I could follow her orders again!"

Back in the living room, they joined King and Russell on the sofas and overstuffed chairs and dug into the tray of food Maria brought out. Abbi and Will began talking to each other about family matters as the other three began discussing what had to be done on the restaurant project. When Maria called them for lunch several hours later, King noticed Abbie was rocking the sleeping Maddie in the big rocking chair by the fireplace.

"Come with me, Will, and let's get that Port-A-Crib set up in your bedroom so Abbie can eat. You brought another playpen as well, didn't you? That might be a good thing until we see how these babies get along together!"

During lunch, it was decided to take a quick trip up to see the restaurant site. All but Abbie left right after the meal, but she chose to stay behind to help Maria care for the three babies.

Camera in hand, Meli started taking pictures almost as soon as she got out of the car. Since King had parked on the street at the front of the building, she started with a full shot of the entire building, then focused on each window on the first floor and then the corner door. Looking up from across the street, she took several shots of the decretive brickwork on the façade, then the flat roof edge.

All of them moved around the corner then into the back parking lot. As King opened the back door with the key Megan had given him, Meli continued to snap photos. Moving into the dark building, she waited until Russell found the light switch, then continued to take pictures of everything.

"I'm glad I brought my digital camera for this. I would have run out of film long ago using my old camera. Now I just need to put in a new memory chip occasionally."

King said, "And knowing you, I feel sure you have plenty of them with you!"

Russell said, "Watch your step here. These stairs are treacherous. Do you want to start at the top and work down or start in the basement and go up?"

"Humm. I'm thinking you guys will be building from the basement up, so let's do that. Then my files will correspond with the work you are doing and make it easier for me to use the photographs."

As they were slowly going down the rotten steps, she asked, "So, what will this be when you finish?"

"Half will be a small apartment for Megan." King answered. "She is thinking about making the other half another apartment for her Chief or maybe a Restaurant Manager, or perhaps just storage at first."

Will took her arm and said, "Be careful here, Love. You have your camera pasted to your face so you can't see where you are going and almost walked into a half-fallen stud. It's almost like you are still blind!"

"Oh, please! Not that again! I'll be more careful. It's just that this is so interesting, even in this condition. I can't seem to stop snapping shots."

"I am intrigued as well. Although this is not my time period of interest usually, the Archeologist in me can't help but 'feel' the history in this building. Just how old is it, King?"

"According to Megan, this is the oldest area of town, which was settled in the late 1800's, so I would guess this building is about 200 years old."

Meli asked, "Is it safe? I mean, I would hate for Megan to put her money into fixing it up only to have it collapse around her ears!"

King said, "Once we get all the rubble out, we will inspect the walls very carefully and repair any weak spots. It will be almost like rebuilding the Hotel/Retirement home. At least here, there is no fire damage to worry about."

Russell added, "One of the first things we plan to do is hire a company to come and gently pressure wash the exterior. That will help show up the places that may need to be repaired."

"Oh, like the cave on Green Mountain. Just enough pressure to get the dirt off, but not enough to do any damage."

"Yep!"

"O.K., I think I'm finished down here. Next stop, first floor."

King led the way up and stopped on the landing at the first floor. "Meli, may I suggest you use your telephoto lens and just stand here on the steps to take your pictures of all these upper floors? Russell and I found most of the flooring to be so rotten, it's dangerous to walk on. I wouldn't want you to fall through."

"Thanks for the warning, King! Yes, I can do that. I particularly want shots of those two outside doors and several of the large display windows, but my lens will make it easy to do from right here."

And so it went for the rest of the other floors. Then they came to the door that led up to the roof. Hanging on one hinge, it was a bit difficult to open, but the three guys put their shoulders to it and finally succeeded. As Meli stepped out behind Russell, she exclaimed, "Oh, guys! You simply must make this a part of the restaurant! Outdoor dining is the trend now, and I can just see this as a great destination dinning spot for the tourists." Walking over to the edge of the roof, she lifted her camera and took pictures in all directions. "You would definitely need to add a safety rail, but just look at these views! Out over the surrounding countryside in this direction, downtown over there, and over here you can see the river! This would be super cool!"

Once Meli said she had all the "before" pictures she needed, they drove back to the castle, arriving just as the three children were being put into their cribs for the night. Meli and Will gave Mattie a hug, then went into the living room to sit with King. Abbie soon joined them, bringing a tray of snacks with her. After sharing the events of the day, Russell said, "I think I have done about all I can here. I suggest we leave early tomorrow morning if we want to get Will back in time for his first class."

"Yes, I agree." Will said. "I'm still not tenured at the University, so really would not want to miss being there at the beginning of the term."

Good nights were said, and they separated to go to their own rooms. When she reached the door to the room she was now sharing with Will, Meli stopped just inside and looked around with a sad smile on her face.

"What bothering you, Love?" Will asked.

"Not 'bothering me' so much as making me remember all the months I spent in this room not knowing who I was. I am so very glad you knew King and contacted him so Sam could come find me."

"I'm very glad she found you, also! Now, let's get some sleep. We'll have a long day tomorrow. Knowing Russell, he will want to drive until well after sunset!"

Chapter Twelve

KING AND MEGAN HAD good luck in getting crews out to work at the restaurant site. The rubble of rotten walls and floors was cleared out in a week, the basement was sprayed for 'creepy crawly insects' as Megan called them, and the floor and walls went up quickly. There was room for two one-bedroom apartments and Megan had King put them on separate meters so they could be used while the rest of the building was finished. Megan began buying the furniture she needed for her apartment and moved in as soon as the first floor was started so she would have a ceiling in her rooms.

The buildout went very quickly after that, and she was soon planning her Grand Opening. The main floor opened to the street with double doors on the corner, recessed into a notch cut off the corner of the building. Those doors led into a large lobby, with a reservations desk and a glass souvenir cabinet along the front wall. Directly across from the entrance was another set of double doors opening into the ballroom. This room was meant to be used for multiple purposes other than just balls. Lectures, live entertainment events, movies, classes, vender craft sales, and extra seating for the restaurant if a group wanted a private party. Toward the back of the lobby were two elevators and the Restrooms, plus a small area with a couple of sofas, chairs, and potted plants. However, the element that caught everyone's eye as they entered the building was a magnificent stairway starting at the elevators and following the outside wall all the way around the lobby. This stairway continued to follow the outside walls of the public areas all the way up to the top and ended in front of another set of double doors leading out onto the roof dining area.

The very large kitchen, walk-in freezers, and storage areas took up most of the back of the building on the second floor. The front part had a small dance floor with a tiny stage, and tables and booths around the edges. It also had a well-stocked bar dividing the two sections, with large tanks at both ends that were kept filled with fish or lobsters. Guest could pick out their own meal. The third floor was the main restaurant in the back with smaller areas around a U-shaped balcony overlooking the dancing below.

Most of the fourth floor consisted of private rooms for birthday parties, bridal showers, or any small group not wanting to be in the main dining room. From there the large stairway led up and out to the rooftop. There were umbrellas on some of the tables and larger areas covered with canvas sunscreens. The area toward the building next to them had been taken over by multiple hydroponic growing beds. Megan had made up her mind early on to serve the freshest food available and found out that she could do this cheaper if she grew her own. She even hired a trained Hydroponics Gardener to oversee that part of her business and turned the basement area next to her apartment over to him. This is where he raised the fish and lobsters until the were large enough to put in the upstairs tanks. He also started the various vegetables there, transplanting them when necessary to the rooftop garden.

The plans for the Grand Opening were formalized, and invitations sent. King and Abbie answered right away saying they would be there. The rest of their family also said they would come, including Granny Edi! She insisted that Will should drive her car but would not even talk about flying out. Because all of her "grandchildren" knew of her fear of flying, they didn't push the issue. Will packed the big car with luggage, his wife and baby, and helped Granny into the back seat, and drove for four days to get to King's Castle. Since Granny had never seen that either, they left her with Abbie and King while they drove on into the city where the rest of the family had made reservations at one of the nearby hotels. The Big Night was a huge success! Melissa had sent out many of her "Before and After" photograph book and they were big sellers at the souvenir table. Several businessmen made reservations for corporate dinners, as well as private couples wanting to celebrate special occasions.

Megan had seated her uncle at the table with King and Russell, along with herself. As the evening progressed, her uncle finally got around to asking her "So tell me, Meggie, why on earth did you name this beautiful place One Hundred and One? That isn't even the address."

"Oh, Uncle Bill, you helped me name it!"

"ME? How is that?"

"Remember when you first offered me this place? You told me that my brothers would only have to take a few steps to reach your requirements for them to inherit their oil wells, but because I am female, I would have to take one hundred and one steps. If you take the time to count that fabulous stairwell King and Russell put in, you will find that it is exactly one hundred and one steps!"

Uncle Bill just looked at her for a few minutes, then roared with laughter.

"Well, girl, you turned the tables on me this time!"

"Not me, Uncle Bill. King is the one that suggested it after I told him what you said. It did seem the perfect idea, so we played with the plans to make it work out."

"Make it work out? What do you mean?"

King picked up the story. "If you climb up all the way from the lobby to the roof dining area, you will find there are several places where you are not always stepping up. We have at least one section on each floor where you walk on the same level for a distance before you come to more steps. Working out exactly how long those sections had to be and how many were needed was a real headache, let me tell you!"

"And you enjoy this kind of challenge, don't you? You and Russell both seem to put a lot of thought into your projects. They are not just rooms shoved together like some projects I've seen. It appears that the odder the requirements, the better you two make it work."

Russell said, "Sir, you have just quoted my own thoughts when I first got into the building trade. I said then that I didn't want to just put a bunch of square rooms together and call it a house. Partnering with King has made it easier to build the kind of buildings I dreamed of but didn't know quite how to do. What I can't think of, he can. I believe we make a pretty good team."

"I agree! To the point that I want to hire your company for another odd-ball project. I have just made up my mind about something. Megan, can we adjourn to one of those private rooms upstairs when we finish eating? I don't want to cut this wonderful dinner short. The food is too good, but what I have to ask of you two gentlemen is not to be made public for some time yet, so I don't want to get into it just now."

"Of course, you can rent a private room, and I'll only charge you half price!"

At the incredulous look from her uncle, she chuckled and said "Kidding! You go have your business meeting and I'll take the ladies to another of those rooms where they can relax with a cup of tea or something. Even kick off their shoes if they want. But right now, I need to get back into my kitchen to oversee the closing of the first night of business of One Hundred and One. Russell, King, thank you so much for doing this for me. You are welcome here any time—on the house! I'll have someone come to show you upstairs when you finish eating."

Chapter Thirteen

THE DELICIOUS MEAL WAS finished with a lot of laughter and joking. One waitress and a busboy came to clear the table and the manager himself came to show them upstairs. He left, telling the ladies there would be tea sent up and other refreshments if wanted, and the guys were offered a drink on the house from the bar.

After he left, Mr. Travis got right down to business.

"As you probably have heard from Megan, I have used my oil business ties to move into the political arena somewhat. Oh, I'll never run for an office. That is just not my style. However, I am one of those people who "knows people in high places". The people who are my friends now are what is also known as "the movers and shakers" and I tend to hear what some of those moves are going to be before they become public knowledge. One of those moves could benefit your company if you care to join forces with me and what I have in mind.

"King, I know you remember all that open land on the other side of my sister's ranch, down toward the river. It's about one thousand acres I believe. Well, I have just learned that our state has a plan for it that involves putting in an interstate highway system and developing the river area as a vacation spot. As I said downstairs, this is just in the planning stages, so it may be years before they could make anything happen. My private plan it this. I would like to build a few apartment buildings right along where the interstate might be going and have already contacted the owner of that land. He is willing to sell to me if he gets a share of the rents on the buildings. He said he would rather deal with me than the government and is willing to pay half of what it would cost to put in our own highway system.

"Now, my question to you two, would you be interested in building those apartments, but not make them just square boxes. I want to see something very different."

King spoke up to say "Mr. Travis, I know exactly the acreage you are talking about, but am a bit confused. Doesn't it still belong to the Granger's? How could you, or even the state, build anything if it still belongs to that cranky bunch?"

"Ah, I see you do remember the Granger Gang. That was the name even when I was a boy, and my grandfather told me once that it was a name that fit. It seems that back when this state was just being settled, a family named Granger moved into that land to have access to the river. They used the river to move quickly all the gold they had stolen from banks and pay wagons in several counties. They were a bunch of outlaws on the run but managed to stay safe there by shooting anyone who came onto their property. It now belongs to a descendant of that group, and he is one of the nicest men you could meet. He bought the land legally a long time ago and has been a model citizen for a long time. You probably haven't kept up with him because he isn't up as far as your home very much. His business is further south, so that's where he goes. Anyway,

Gordan is willing to work with us, help build the roadway, and would even like to live in one of the apartments when they are finished."

Russell asked, "So why do you want to cut your friends at the state level out of doing this project?"

"Son, when you have lived as long as I have, and delt with as many businesspeople as I have, you learn that mostly your friends are only friends as long as you can help them do what they want to do. If you have no help to give, they are no longer your friends. Those folks in politics at the state level will talk a lot, debate a lot, try to work out many scams to see how much they can cheat Gordan Granger out of, then probably never complete the project. When I called them my friends, it was a mistake-they are merely acquaintances that I have delt with from time to time. I pick my true friends more carefully than that and call many men AND women my friends and really mean it. From what I have seen, and what I have heard from my sister, I think the three of us could be friends and work together well. I know this is a lot to think about and you probably need so time to think about it. I will be visiting my sister at the Circle M for the next few days. She asked me tonight, and I thought it might be a good idea. Now that I've given you two something to think about, I want to be close enough to hear the answer."

"As you said, this is a lot to think about, and I'm sure there will be many questions. Russell is staying here in one of the hotels, but we talk a lot over the phone. He can come down to The Castle when Granny Edi and Will go back East. She is staying in our guest room right now. As soon as he is down there, we will get in touch with you."

"Sounds good. Those phones work all the way out to The Circle M too, you know. Don't hesitate to call and ask those questions."

"We might do that. Right now, I really need to get Granny Edi back so she can get to bed. It's been a long day for her. Thank you for thinking Russell and I could handle this project. He and I will talk it to death in the next couple of days and contact you soon."

The three gentlemen rose and went next door to collect their wives and Granny. While most of them walked the few blocks to their hotel, King made sure Granny was buckled into the back seat, pulled out a pillow and blanket for her, then he and Abbie settled in for the twenty-mile trip back to The Castle.

Chapter Fourteen

EARLY THE NEXT MORNING while they were waiting for the twins to wake up, Abbie took Granny on a tour of the Castle, even down on the ground floor where they were in the process of making the playground/pool area. Settling in the living room later with a cup of coffee, Granny told King how much she had enjoyed seeing what he had done "with this big pile of rocks". I may not be able to SEE what you have done here, but Abbie explained everything so well I felt I could visualize all of it.

"Of course, it isn't just a pile of rocks, is it. These walls seem very firmly in place and not shifting around at all like separate rocks would do. You can be very proud of what you have done here. And that fancy restaurant we were in last night! You and Russell outdid yourselves on that one. Any idea what you two will attempt next?"

"Actually, I'm just waiting until the others get here before I tell you and Abbie. We have had an offer, but I need to talk to Russell to find out just how much we will be able to tell you about it."

Abbie asked, "I suppose that is what Megan's uncle wanted to talk to you about last night?"

"Right! And he said to not spread the information around until we decide if we will join him on the adventure or not. If Russell and I go with him, we can fill you in. If we don't, you may or may not hear of it on the news."

"Well, that is certainly mysterious! I hope Russell gets here soon!"

Abbie said "I hear the elevator right now, Granny, so we may hear right away. While they come in and get settled, I'll go ask Marie to bring in more coffee, and maybe some of her sweet rolls."

The whole Melrose Farm gang was seated in the living room when Maria appeared with the rolls, closely followed by Squire carrying a large tray with cups, saucers, and a large pot of coffee.

Granny Edi looked around at all of her "grandchildren" as they spoke and smiled. She felt she had been very blessed when these young people came into her life and then became one family. She was a tiny bit partial to Will of course, since he was her own late daughter's child, but still loved all the others as well.

The sweet rolls were gone and the coffee getting cold, so Russell turned to King and said "Hey, Bro, don't you think we need to talk in your office?"

King put down his cup and stood. "Yes, we do. Are you still thinking along the same lines as you were when we talked on the phone before sunup this morning?"

"Pretty much. I still have questions, so maybe a call to Mr. Travis should move to the top of our agenda."

They moved off down the hall to King's office, still talking, but not even saying anything to the others. No one thought anything about that, they were used to those two when they were talking 'business'.

Abbie said to Will "Are you still planning to leave for the East this afternoon?"

"Yes, I am. Duty calls you know, I need to be back in the classroom one week from yesterday. My temporary replacement has another job lined up right after that. If we leave today, I will not have to push so hard to get back in time."

Jeff spoke up to say "Sam and I will be flying out this afternoon also. We'll hold down the fort until you guys get back."

"Sam added "I can't wait to hear all the tales about our animals. I'm sure Granny's friend has several by now! It was so nice of her to volunteer to look after them for us."

Just then the other two guys came back in. Russell went directly to Katie and gave her a big hug.

"Uh-o, what do you need to do that I'm not going to like?"

"Ummm, well, it's like this, Love. Megan's uncle Travis has offered King and me a fantastic opportunity, but I need to be here a couple of days longer to meet with him and someone else to really decide if we want to do this or not. Would you want to stay or fly back with Sam and Jeff?"

"Oh, bother! You are always letting my brother talk you into things!"

King said "Not so, Sister mine! This time it was Russell who thought we should hear more of what Mr. Travis has to say."

"Then Susan and I are going home with Sam and Jeff. You stay here as long as you need to find out about this new adventure."

Russell and King were all smiles, but it was Abbi who stood up and called for everyone's attention."

"Because the whole family is here, except for Doc Simmons of course, there is something King and I would like for you to know. It appears the twins are going to have to share us with an addition to the family in about five months!"

The room erupted with excitement. There was a lot of hugging and backslapping and talk of names and what would be needed. Things were just slowing down and becoming calmer when Jeff moved to Sam's side, picked up her hand, gave her a look, then said "Just so you know, Sam and I will add another cousin to the mix about the same time!"

It took a few minutes for that to sink in, but then the room erupted again. It was a very happy group that moved into the dining room when Maria called them to lunch.

Chapter Fifteen

AFTER KING SAID GOODBYE to Will, Meli, and Granny Edi, then drove Sam, Jeff, and Katie with Susan to the airport, he and Russell went directly to the Circle M. Mr. Travis met them at the front door, invited them into the ranch office and closed the door.

"Well, Gentlemen, the fact that you are here leads me to believe you are at least a little bit interested in this project. However, I'm sure you still have many questions, so let's begin.

King started with "So Gordan Granger wants to be a big part of this? I think Russell and I need to meet him before we go too much further. Could we set up a time to do that?"

"No need! I already asked him to meet us here. He should be arriving any time now. Even if you two decided not to join us, there were some issues he and I needed to talk over. I will push forward with this plan even if I have to go with another architectural firm."

Looking out of the office window he added "Ah! There he is now. Excuse me while I go let him in."

The man that entered the room looked nothing like an outlaw or part of a gang. He was clean shaven, had on what looked to be a custom-made business suit, and carried what

King recognized as a very expensive Stetson hat in his hand that matched his very expensive Western boots.

Mr. Travis said "Gordan, I'd like you to meet Sebastian Cole, better known as King, and Russell Mayhew, the two geniuses that built Megan's restaurant. King, Russell, this is Gordan Granger, better known a little further south as "Mr. Saddles".

"Is that you!" King practically shouted. "Every saddle on my brother Bob's ranch came from your store! Russell, you have several back at Melrose Farm that came from there and I will not purchase from anywhere else. Good to meet you in person, Mr. Granger."

"Please call me Gordan. If we are to be working together on this project, we can't stand on ceremony. Bill, you did say you thought these guys wouldn't be able to turn down this project, didn't you?"

Bill Travis said, "I think what I actually said was 'they would be pretty stupid to do so'. No offence meant. But we are getting a little ahead of ourselves here. Gordan, why don't you explain what you and I have been talking about for the last six months or so?"

"Well, to give you the story of my life in as few words as possible, my mother and grandmother did not want me to follow in my father's and grandfather's footsteps, which were not always on the right side of the law. They scrimped and saved every penny they could earn legally by moving into town and taking in laundry to send me to school. I graduated from high school and went on to college part time while I worked as an apprentice with a saddle maker. When he retired, he left the business to me. I hired others to make the saddles and the reins and other tack while I used my college classes in Business Administration to market those products. The rest, as some people would say, is history. I've done very well, and now would like to give some of that back.

"When Bill came to my office wanting to talk about the property I own along the river, I got rather angry at first, thinking he was from the state. You see, back when I was trying to buy that land my ancestors had claimed, the state put up multiple roadblocks to keep me from doing it. 'It belonged to the Native Americans.' 'It was zoned improperly.' 'I was claiming too much land.' Just one excuse after another, until I hired a good attorney and we pushed it through. Now the state is thinking about trying to buy it back and turning it into an overdeveloped tourist attraction. I want to work with Bill to see that doesn't happen, and I hope you will help."

Russell asked, "What do you envision as the end goal for this property?"

"I would like to see it turned into a sort of wilderness park, but with amenities such as a few nice apartments or even some private homes, shops, entertainment, and museums right along with the nature trails and animal sighting tours and take advantage of the beautiful river for water sports. I am prepared to foot the bill for the access roads, our own "interstate" if you will, to connect this property to the surrounding cities. A tourist attraction, yes, but a place where people could live year-round if they wish."

King asked, "Exactly how much acreage are we talking about and what would you want us to do?"

"It is just over one thousand acres. Bill and I would want your company to design and build all the buildings on the property. Every one of them! Bill tells me you do the unusual with your projects, and that is exactly what I am looking for. I would like to see even the boathouse on the river or the tour guide office to be special. Nothing glitzy or ostentatious, but different than what one would expect."

"I think Russell and I need to see this property before we commit to anything. How would you feel about an aerial tour this afternoon?"

Bill said "Aerial tour? I'm not sure we could arrange one so quickly."

"We don't have to. I'll use the small plane Bob keeps at the ranch. All we would have to do is fuel her up!"

"Then let's go!"

Chapter Sixteen

AN HOUR LATER, RUSSELL exclaimed "This is beautiful land! I can see why you would not want it over developed. The fewer buildings the better if you want to keep the wilderness look. Those high hills to the West are just begging for hiking trails and I see a herd of antelope on that lower one. This would take a lot of planning and mapping out to take full advantage of the potential."

King added "Russell and I could certainly cover the construction of any buildings, but as for everything else you want here, you would have to call in experts in the various fields. For instance, we know nothing about laying out hiking trails or planning water sports activities."

Bill said "We had already come to that conclusion and have started looking into who we need to see. I think the very first thing to do is draw up a map of the whole property and plan where to put everything to make the best use of the acreage. One thousand acres sounds like a lot, but it can get eaten up quickly when you start putting structures on it."

Gordan said "I already have a topical map in my office. We can see all those hills and exactly how high they are. We had planned to contact a Park Ranger friend of Bill's to help with laying out those trails."

"Can we get a copy of that map and mark out where you want to put the main road?" King was beginning to sound very excited."

Gordan said. "A representative from the state has already contacted me once. I would like to have this settled before she calls me again. Do you guys think you would want to be a part of this? If so, we need a planning session right away to get the contracts drawn up."

King looked at Russell, got an affirmative nod, then said to the other two "Why don't we plan to meet in my office at The Castle tomorrow morning about ten o'clock? That way I can show you photographs of some of our other projects. If you still like what you see, then I believe Russell and I will be working with you for several months!"

"Works for me." Gordan said. "I'll bring several copies of my map so we can start planning the layout."

Bill said "I am very pleased with how this is working out. Gordan has the land, Mayhew-Cole Construction has the expertise, and I have the contacts and some of the money. We can't lose!"

Breakfast the next morning was lively conversation from start to finish. Abbi was very interested in hearing about the project, promised to keep the twins occupied during the meeting, and asked if there was anything else she could do.

King answered "Well, as a matter of fact, we don't have anyone to sit in and take notes. Could you ask Maria to watch the babies and play Secretary for us? Hiring one should be high on our list of things to do, but right now, we will make do with your feeble efforts."

"Will you just listen to him, Russell? As many times as I have taken notes for him, and he says that about me!"

"You know I'm just joking with you, my Love. You are a very good secretary. But we do need to think of getting a permanent one."

"What about Kelly in your office here in the village? Didn't you say she has learned about all you could teach her"

"You are right!" Turning to Russell he said "Kelly came to work for us on a work-study assignment from the community college here in town. I would hire her, but my Jennifer is really all I need. Excuse me a few minutes, and I'll see if she can come out today."

"So, Russell, tell me more about this new project. You and King seem to be very excited about it, but I'm not quite clear about what it involves.

"Funny you should say that! I'm not sure any of the four of us really know all that it will turn out to be. It seems to get bigger every time we talk about it! Basically, one of the partners, Gordan Granger, has a good bit of land he wants to develop into a sort of park, but one where people could live if they want to. Megan's Uncle Travis heard on the "political grapevine" that the state wanted to buy up that land and put in a large development, not saving any of it for recreational use.

"He and Gordan got together to form a plan completely different, and now they want King and me to build all the buildings needed. It could turn out to be a very expensive project to build, but one that would give good returns in the long run. I am seriously considering the possibility of buying a share in the company. I'll have to talk to Katie about that. Which reminds me. With the time change, I had put off calling to share all this, but she should be awake by now. Excuse me, please."

Just then King came back into the room and said that Kelly should be arriving about the same time as the other two, so Abbie would not have to be Secretary after all.

Abbie said "This must be a very special project! Russell was just telling me he may want to buy in as a shareholder in the company. Is it really that good?"

"Abbie, this could be one of the best things to happen to us. Buying a share may be a very good idea. Wait a minute! Shares! I think I just thought of another way to handle this! I'll be in my office when people show up." And he practically ran out of the room.

Russell came back a few minutes later, then followed King to the office when Abbie told him where King had gone.

Kelly arrived first and was shown to the office. She was soon followed by Bill and Gordan. As soon as they had all been shown to the office, Abbie asked Maria to carry in coffee, then went to play with her twins.

King was standing behind his desk sifting through photograph albums on the bookcase against the wall. Turning as he heard the door opening, he said "Come on in!" Waving a hand toward Kelly he stated "I took the liberty of inviting Kelly to be here to act as Secretary for this meeting. Let's look at the photos first, as they may make you change your mind about hiring our construction firm."

Grabbing a cup of coffee and indicating the others should also, he moved aside so the others could see the books. After going over just a few of the photos, Gordan said "These convince me you guys are just what I want for this project. What you did with that old hotel is amazing. Shall we get down to hammering out a contract?"

"One thing I would like to suggest before we get to that." King put his coffee cup on the tray, then turned to them and said "While chatting with Abbie this morning, a thought hit me. Gordan, you say you would like to see this property turned into a sort of recreational park and community where people could live if they wanted to. But if you have us build only single-family homes, or even 'for sale' apartments you would soon not own any of it except the recreational areas! What would you and Bill think about turning this whole project into a Time-Share Resort? There could still be nice-looking apartments and a few single-family units, shops, recreational areas, indeed, all those amenities you wanted, but the land itself would still belong to you."

Silence. The only sound was Kelly's keys clicking on her laptop. Then even that sound stopped while she waited for someone to say something.

Still silence. Suddenly, two people spoke at once.

"I like that idea!" from Bill.

"What a wonderful plan!" from Gordan. "It wouldn't necessary change how we want to build it out but would assure a return on our investment far into the future."

"If this is the direction it's going, I would like to buy into the company as an investor, not just a part of the construction team." Russell said.

"As would I." King echoed. "Can we draw up the contract to include Russell and me as co-partners with you two in this adventure?"

"That would be fine with me. How do you feel about it, Gordan?"

"Let's do it! If we can get the main ideas down today, I'll take the notes to my attorney and let him draw up a proper contract. As soon as that is done, we can get serious about laying out all the elements."

"Maybe we can also get started today on a list of all the things you said you wanted." King pulled out a small notebook from his pocket and began flipping through it. Bill smiled when he saw that Russell had done the same thing. "We should probably have some idea about what we will have to find room for on those thousand acres!"

Russell spoke up to say "I have a longer list than he does. He was busy flying the plane!"

"But mine is even longer!" Gordan said as he pulled a file from his briefcase.

The next several hours were spent comparing the lists, adding to, and sometimes deleting items. At the end of that time, Russell said "Well, Gordan, it looks like King and I may have to double up on some of these buildings and make them serve two functions to have some free space. But we can play around with that later. Right now, I have another suggestion to add. How about a riding stable for the guests? I believe it is something almost necessary for a Time Share Resort these days. Planed out correctly, they could use the same trails as the hikers."

"Good! I like that idea." Gordan said.

"O.K. here's another one for you." King said. "How about putting in a small landing strip? Most of your guests will be fairly well off financially and may like to fly in their own planes for their vacations."

Gordan said, "I like that idea also, but no more suggestions until we find out how much of these things we can actually fit in. We have accomplished a great deal today, and I'm looking forward to working with all of you in the coming months. Kelly, is this just a fill-in position for this meeting only, or would you be available to work for this group on a permanent basis?"

She turned to look at King, and he answered for her. "Kelly's contract with me is over at the end of next week. Where she works after that is completely up to her. I will say that my Jennifer has trained her well and Kelly would have my blessing if she chose to work for this group."

"You know, Kelly's situation just brought up another thing we need to think about." Bill said. "I believe we need to set up a working office closer to the site since we are going to be there a lot. Maybe haul in a small trailer as office space for a while.

Gordan said "No need to do that. There is one of the original cabins left from my great-grandparent's day right beside the river. I had planned to turn it into the museum if enough of it can be saved, but it could work as office space for the time being. There is even a small room attached to the back that Kelly could use as a bedroom until we can build better quarters for her. That's assuming she will take the job, of course."

Everyone turned to look at Kelly. She blushed beet red but was able to studder an acceptance to their offer. "I didn't think finding a job would be this easy! Thank all of you so much. Ummm, may I take my cat?"

All the men roared with laughter, shaking their heads as they packed up their notes. Russell said to all of them "I suggest we go down there tomorrow and see what will be needed. We will, of course, need a desk, a couple of chairs, file cabinets, etc., but I'm thinking more about physical comfort. Is that cabin air conditioned? Is there a working bathroom? Cooking facilities? We are pretty much starting from scratch here and I can see lots of 'things-to-do-lists' before we even start on building out the park!"

"I agree, Russell." Bill said. "I intend to order up all the office furniture and supplies, but there will be a lot of other things needed. Let's meet at the property at ten tomorrow and get a start on those to-do lists!"

"You too, Kelly." King said. "Shall I pick you up at my office downtown about nine? There are some papers I would like to have from there, and then you can ride down with Russell and me this first time. After that, you will need to have your car down there."

The meeting broke up, handshakes given and received, Bill, Gordan, and Kelly went home, and King and Russell went to the living room to collapse into the easy chairs with big sighs. Abbie came in a few minutes later and said to them "Can I assume from the satisfied smiles on your faces you had a good meeting? Is the project for Mr. Travis a done deal?"

"Even more than just a project for Mr. Travis, love. Russell and I will be partners with Bill Travis and Gordan Granger to build an entire Time Share Resort! The potential earnings from this could mean an early retirement for both of us."

"You're kidding! An entire vacation Resort? It could take years to build everything needed for that!"

"We will start slowly and hire in others for some of the attractions such as hiking trails and such, but they want Mayhew-Cole to build all of the buildings. Kelly has been hired as our secretary, and we are all meeting at the site tomorrow to make more plans."

Looking over at Russell, Abbie commented "You don't look as happy about this as King. What is your objection?"

"Oh, no objection to this partnership at all. I am very well pleased with it and agree with King that it could be the best thing since sliced bread for our future financial security. I'm just not looking forward to telling Katie how much time I will have to be here rather than at home."

"Oh! Yes, I can see where that would be a problem. Just tell her that both of you are always welcome here for however long you must stay. And who knows, when you get the first units up, she might enjoy staying at a Resort for a week or so!"

"Well, there is that! Depending on what other amenities are functional by then. I hope…"

Just then Maria came into the room to announce the meal, so they all went into eat.

Chapter Seventeen

"To continue that thought, I was going to say I hope we can get most of the preliminary's out of the way today. Then I can get back home, give my ladies a big hug, then do some of the design work there. Just make sure your FAX machine works, King!"

"And that might be one of the first things we ask Bill to order for the office on site. I can see it being used often. Eat quickly. If we are to pick up Kelly on time, we need to leave here in about ten minutes."

Abbie said "I am going down to the ranch to talk to Ruth this morning. She wants to start her Handicap Horseback lessons as soon as the special saddles come in, so I need to know what I am supposed to do."

King looked at Abbie rather strangely, then asked "Do you happen to know where she ordered those saddles?"

"Some company Bob suggested. 'Mr. Saddles' I think it's called."

King and Russell burst out laughing, then told Abbie the joke!

"Gordan Granger owns that company! Wait until I tell him my sister-in-law is using one of his special products."

They left, picked up Kelly, and made good time reaching the cabin on the river. Travis and Gordan were already there, pacing around the outside and shaking their heads at what they saw. It was a mess! A hole in the roof, half of the porch falling, the front door hanging by one hinge, and the whole yard was waist high in weeds.

"I haven't been out here in years. It always brought back too many bad memories, and that is one reason I wanted to do something special with the property—to change those bad memories into good ones. Well, this can all be repaired quickly and will do until we can get something else built, IF the inside is still usable. Let's go see."

Forcing the door open, they stopped just inside to let their eyes get used to the darkness. Everything was covered in dust blowing through the broken windows, there was no furniture except one broken chair, and the small sink on one side of the back door was partially falling off the wall.

Looking around, Gordan said "I don't remember it being this bad, but Momma, Gram, and I left here when I was seven years old. There is no running water yet but there is a well just outside that we can tap. A generator will give us electricity, and we can put up a wall to make a small bath in the back room. I remember Momma fighting hard for that kitchen sink to be put in. She wanted to be "civilized", but that was the only thing Poppa and Gramps would agree to. My uncles laughed at them for doing that much, so they wouldn't put in anymore "civilized frippery's". Soon after that, Momma had had enough and moved us into town."

Bill said "Kelly, does your laptop have enough battery power to take a few notes?"

"Yes, Sir. I made sure it was fully charged before I left home this morning."

"O.K. I would like for you to find a cleaning service willing to come this far out and get this place scrubbed down. Then start looking up anything you can find on Time Shares and how to run them. King, can you call in one of your construction crews to make a few repairs here? Kelly, while you are on the computer, look up a company that will come out and cut all these weeds. Gordan, how is the contract coming? Will we be able to sign it today?"

King chuckled and said "Well, I can see how you got so far in your business ventures! You just jump in and start getting things done. That is exactly how Russell and I do things. Gordan, I will assume you are pretty much the same since you have done so well making saddles. Oh! That reminds me. My Abbie told me this morning that she was going to the ranch to get some training with a special saddle made for teaching handicap youngsters. My sister-in-law Ruth Cole is going to start a business doing that as soon as her saddles arrive from the company. Want to guess where they are coming from?"

Gordan looked at him for a few minutes, then pulled out his cell phone and pushed a few buttons. "Emily, look up the order for a Mrs. Ruth Cole for handicap saddles and mark it PAID IN FULL. See that the order is shipped as soon as possible. I'll be back in the office right after lunch. Bye."

As the others looked at him with their mouths hanging open, he said "What? Can't I be a "Good Guy" occasionally? I hope my ancestors are spinning in their graves! I love to do things that would have made them angry! King, the contract should be finished today, and we can sign it tomorrow. Now, let's look at the topo maps and decide where the best place would be to put the access road."

A few more hours of work, a few more instructions to Kelly, and they all headed off to other errands. After dropping Kelly off near her car, King and Russell headed back to The Castle.

Russell said "After all the progress we made today I think I'll plan to start back East as soon as we get the contract signed. You and the others will be tied up with getting the first steps done, and I can work from there just as well as I could here."

"You are correct, but I'll miss having you here to bounce ideas off. I can see a lot of long-distance phone calls in our future.

"Yep! Say, I wonder what Maria has for lunch."

"We'll find out soon! I'm parking on the driveway ramp and taking the elevator up. It's quicker that way."

The contract was signed the next day, the location of the access road was finalized, and Bill called the company that had put roads out to some of his remote oil wells to come do the work. They decided that the first building to be built on the property was a Duplex Condo for the Time Share guests. King had convinced the rest that several "Villages" of groups of these units would be a great start to the whole project. He drew a quick outline of his vision of what it should look like and got their approval. It would be two very nice one-story houses built together, with a garage for each in the middle, a deck on the back to take advantage of the views, and best of all, would serve as a better temporary office on one side plus give any visiting family, friends, or businesspeople a nice place to stay on the other side.

When they got home that evening, Russell told Abbie he would not be going out to the site the next day but would be heading back East instead. He would send King the rough draft of the plans for the inside of the new units as soon as possible. Meanwhile, King would start gathering his crew and ordering materials for building the first unit. Gordan and Bill were going to be busy planning and having the first of the utilities put in, one "village" at the time.

Two months later, after pushing his crew to work 16-hour days/6 days a week, it was finished, inspected by Bill and Gordan, approved, and Kelly moved into the office side, using one of the bedrooms for herself and the other bedroom for storage of office supplies. The living room/dining area was the main office, and she always had a pot of coffee brewing in the small but fully equipped kitchen. Gordan made the decision that the old office was just not worth saving, so it was torn down and plans were made to put a small museum in another location later. Kelly was still researching how Time Share Resorts were managed and was told to start contacting the people needed to do the various jobs. Housekeeping staff, Lawn services, Building militance, and on and on and on. The "Interstate" access road was completed, and looked just like any other interstate, with a large circular interchange about one third of the way from one side of the property. It went from one city to another, joining with the Interstates already there. Where the roads peeled off at the interchange, one was the main road that led deeper into the park and the other led out to the small airport built along the border of the property.

One evening King had brought a handful of plans into the dinning room so he could spread them out on the table. When Abbie asked him why he was frowning so, he told her "I just keep coming back to these plans for the road. Gordan's "Interstate". Very impressive and super access to our Resort but taking up all that land just bugs me. The circular interchange alone could be another whole "Village" with rental units."

She walked over to see the plans and studied them a few minutes. "Yes, I see what you mean. That is one big Four-Leaf Clover with a lot of open ground in the "leaves". Too bad you can't build there within the road barriers. I'm going to go get the twins ready for bed. Want to help?"

"Sure. I'll be right there. Just let me stack up these papers and get them back into my office."

Abbie was just changing Rona when he came in, muttering to himself. It sounded like 'stack up' and 'leaves' and 'road barrier', but she couldn't be sure. He started to change Ren, but suddenly stopped with one of his son's feet in the jammies and the other one waving in the air. "Take over here, Abbie! I have just come up with the perfect plan so there won't be any wasted space! Thank you for giving me the idea." And he was gone.

Chapter Eighteen

WHEN KING PITCHED HIS 'perfect plan' to Bill and Gordan, the older Bill thought he had let the strain of the past few months get to him.

"You have completely lost your good sense, King!" Bill said. "This is completely unheard of! Building in the middle of the road? What are you thinking?"

"Well, it's not really in the middle of the road, as the road would go around the building, but it is a way to take advantage of open land that would otherwise be unusable."

"Wow! When Bill told me you had far out ideas for Megan's restaurant, he wasn't kidding! This is brilliant, and just the different look I want for the whole Resort. But can you really do this? Aren't there rules or something?"

"I will have to double check, but I believe as long as the building doesn't actually cover any part of the road, it is legal."

"All right, explain this to me again. Maybe this time it will make more since." Bill was unconvinced, but willing to listen.

"Let's look at the map for a minute." King spread out the topo map on the table. "Here is the two-lane road heading North. Here and here, there is an exit lane so people can get off the Interstate. The same thing is true on the other side heading South. A two-lane road with two exit lanes. All these exits are necessary to give guests access to our Resort. Abbie said this interchange looks like a big Four-Leaf Clover. Then she said it was to bad I couldn't build 'on the leaves'. Then she had to go take care of our babies and I started stacking up my papers to take them back to my office. It was later that I put it all together. By building tall, "stacked" circular buildings on all four "leaves" we will have four nice apartment buildings without taking up even more acreage."

Gordan asked "Would the apartment towers be connected to each other in any way?"

"I suppose we could plan them that way. Why?"

"It just hit me while I was listening to you. If these four towers could be connected in some way, we could have a complete city inside the Resort, without taking up a lot of space. For instance, one tower for apartments, one for a shopping mall, maybe one for business offices with a nice restaurant on the top floor. If this worked out, we could build another complex just like it, but with only apartments in all the towers. Our Resort could triple the availability for rentals without using too much land that could be used for activities. And this way, we could rent out some of the apartments by the year instead of by the week. People could live here year-round if they want to."

"By golly, I'm liking this idea more and more! Where do we go from here?"

King said "I will have to get Russell involved. Usually, the way we work is I design the outside and he does the inside. Designing interiors for a circular building may be a bit of a challenge, but I'm sure he is up to it. We will have to get the measurements for those "clover leaves" as soon as possible. To the inch! Then I can start in the outside of the towers. Now, we need to decide if we want to dig a basement and use it as a parking garage for the tenants. We could then tunnel under the roads to give access to the rest of the property and to all the other towers. I think I should probably concentrate on one tower first, then correct anything that doesn't work when I design the others. And while I'm at it, I'm going to look at the smaller sections between the exit roads and the main roads. It's not enough to build an apartment, but I can probably think of something to put there. We are going to save so much land we might have enough left over for a golf course!"

Just then Kelly called out "Lunch!"

She had started fixing casseroles at night soon after she moved into the new office. For herself at first but was soon making enough to feed all of them at noon.

Gordan came and sat down, then asked "Kelly, where do you get the groceries for your meals? I don't mean to be personal, but this goes along with what we were just talking about for the Resort."

"I shop when I go home on the weekends, then bring it back. I even bought a cooler to keep my milk and butter and stuff cold on the trip back."

"King, add a grocery store in one of those towers!"

"I have another question for you, Kelly." Bill took another bite of the chicken pot pie, swallowed, then asked "With the way this project is growing very quickly, are you getting overwhelmed with all the work we are piling on you? Do you think hiring a bookkeeper would lighten the load enough, so you don't start pulling out your hair?"

"Well, sir, I'm doing O.K. so far, but I do a lot of work at night after all of you gentlemen leave to go home. Most of that is the bookkeeping, I'll admit. If we can afford it, having someone else working here would be a delight. Not only to take some of the work load off my shoulders, but the company would be nice also."

"Done. Put an ad in the paper tomorrow. Speaking of the newspaper, should we start having one delivered here every day?"

King said "Yes, ask them to do that when you call to place the ad for a bookkeeper. Bill, if you can get the measurements from the company that put in the roads, I'll leave you guys to do your thing and go home and do mine. Russell and I have a long conversation ahead of us."

Gordan stopped King as he was going out the door. "A moment of your time, please. I assume you keep the plans of all the buildings you have built? I mean I'm sure you still have the full plans for this first one, since we plan to add others to this Village."

"Yes. Where are you going with this?"

"After talking about having some year-to-year leases so that The Resort will also be a permanent community, I have decided I would like to give up my apartment in town and have you build a permeant home here for me. Just like this one but make it one house instead of two. I may even move my business office here when you get those towers built!"

"Your house will be easy enough. Just tell me where you want it and make sure the utilities go that far. We can even get a good start on it while the plans for all the towers are being drawn up. I'll redraw the original plans to turn it into one house tonight, after I talk to Russell."

The first thing King did when he reached home was send Russell a copy of the interchange, blown up so he could write in measurements.

He told Abbie "Yep, that's all I sent right now. Let him wonder what it's all about, then I'll have fun explaining when I call after dinner. How are you feeling, love? Morning sickness is still bothering you I know. I heard you this morning."

"I'm fine. Maria makes sure I have a good supply of crackers close by and that helps. She is also beginning to boss me around when she thinks I am doing too much. When you talk to Russell, be sure to ask how Sam is doing. You know how close we got when I lived there, and I worry about her. It's almost as if we really were sisters."

"Abbie, you just take care of yourself and don't worry about Sam. Her husband is a doctor you know. I'm sure your brother is looking after her very well, and she has Katie and Granny Edi too. Plus, Granny Edi's friend Molly and Doc Simmons."

"Yes, you're right. I'm just being silly. Ruth was telling me the same thing when I went to see her yesterday. Oh, did you know what your Mr. Granger did? Or should I say, "Mr. Saddles"? He did not charge her one penny for the special handicap saddles. She wrote to thank him right away of course, but could you tell him how much it meant to her? But why "Mr. Saddles". That is such a silly name!"

"He told us it was what people called the man who left the business to him, so he kept it to honor his mentor."

King quickly finished his dinner, gave Abbie a kiss, and went into his office. As expected, there was a piece of paper waiting for him on the FAX. Not very politely worded, either!

He sat down at his desk and pushed the 'quick dial' for Russell's phone.

"So, you didn't understand why I sent you a picture of a road? I thought it was perfectly obvious."

"Oh, yea? What am I not seeing?"

"Four apartment towers built in the open areas next to the exit lanes."

"What?"

"O.K. So we have a four-lane divided highway going North and South. On our Resort property, there are exit and access roads coming off that and going East and West, one out to the airstrip and the other going deeper into the Resort. This makes what Abbie called a Four-Leaf Clover. She suggested it was a shame we could not make use of that space to build apartments. I think I've found a way to do just that. We will build them UP, using the footprint of the surrounding hard service roads as the outer wall boundary of the towers."

"Fascinating concept! Is it legal?"

"Gordan has his legal team looking into that as I speak. He has even suggested that we use the different towers for different uses. One residential, another a mall, another one devoted to business offices. He would like to see an entire city on the Resort, with some year-to-year leases along with the vacation rentals. He has already asked me to build a permanent house for him out there, using the original building plans, but making his one house instead of two."

"Woah! It sounds as if you guys have really done some brainstorming since I left. So, as usual, you are leaving the interior design to me? That will be a challenge, but it sounds like fun. I have a small project to finish up here, then I can start on that. By then you should know if it is legal to build that close to the road.

"Sam just asked me to ask how is Abbie feeling? All is well, I hope."

"All good, and Abbie asked about Sam. Is she over the morning sickness deal yet?"

"She is great and has even taken on a project at the hospital."

"Oh? What kind of project?"

"Remember those awful plastic chairs in the waiting areas? She has started a fundraising campaign to re-do all the waiting rooms, not only with new chairs, but vending machines as well."

"Sounds like a worthwhile endeavor but tell her to take it easy."

"Don't worry, Jeff and Doc are watching her very carefully, as is Granny Edi. She says she can tell by the sound of Sam's voice when she is getting tired, so can then boss her into taking a nap!"

"And speaking of naps, it's about time for me to 'suggest' one to Abbie. We'll keep in touch about the tower project. Talk to ya' later, Bro."

Chapter Nineteen

THE GROUP WAS TOLD that since the road interchange was completely on private property, they could build anything they wanted in the free space. King was seen walking around and around in those open spaces, and even flew the ranch plane over the area to see what the views from the towers might offer. Gordan had made up his mind to put his house about halfway up on one of the lower hills to the West, facing the river. The underground utilities had been run out there and the building supplies delivered. King's construction crew already had the foundation in and planned to begin the framing the following week.

King was sitting at one of the desks in the corporation office, drawing out ideas for the towers while sipping a cup of coffee Kelly had placed in front of him when Bill came blustering in and stomped over to sit in the other chair.

"Fools! Blasted fools, that's what they are! Now I have to go straighten out their mess!"

"Excuse me?"

"Oh, sorry, King. Not anyone here, thank goodness. All the companies I've hired to do work here are doing just what they are supposed to. No, it's those fools out at my oil field north of the city. They just called me and said the new pipe won't be delivered until I sign for it. Something about "not trusting" my foreman. That man has been working for me for fifteen years, and never had a problem. It's the new pipe supplier that is causing the problem. I must go up and crack some heads together and may be gone a few days. I'll be stopping by to see Megan on my way back. Any messages?"

"Yes, as a matter of fact. With these new towers, I am always trying to come up with ideas of what we should have in them, and Gordan mentioned early on about putting a restaurant on the top floor of one of them. I wonder if Megan would be interested in opening a second location here. It would probably not be until early next year, but she could be thinking about it."

"O.K. I'll pass it on. And will you pass on to Gordan he should not purchase any paint from that wholesaler that came by last week. I've found another source that will give us a better discount. See you in a few days. A week at the most. Bye."

Because these towers were going to be a very prominent part of the Resort and the first thing guests would see when they drove that way, King wanted them to be as perfect as possible. He spent many hours both at home and on-site drawing and re-drawing plans. He was finally pleased with the finished drawings and could hardly wait for Bill to get back so they could go over them and approve or disapprove. Gordan had peaked over his shoulder several times, offered suggestions, and seemed to like what he saw. Finally, Bill came back, and early the next morning the three of them took a pot of coffee, a pan of cinnamon buns Kelly had made, and shut themselves up in the garage of the office unit. They had moved a large table and several chairs in there long ago and used it as a Board Room or a place to interview potential contractors. Each of them poured a cup of coffee, grabbed a napkin and cinnamon bun, and settled around the table.

Bill said "King, you're up. Show us your plans."

Spreading out the drawings, King said "The first thing you will notice is that I have used our native sandstone for the siding, just like on this building. As you know, I live in a sandstone cave, and found it to be a very good insulator. Heating in the winter will not be much of a problem here, but I feel the sandstone will give a good barrier to the high temperatures in summer. That way, we will not have to have such thick insulation in the walls, which will mean thinner walls by an inch or two, and give the interior a few more inches, cumulatively speaking, to turn into usable space.

"I have not put balconies on any of the towers, as that would make them hang over the roads. However, I have used very large, floor-to-ceiling windows all around, with sliding doors. Opened, those doors will make the entire room a balcony. I have indicated a guard rail on the outside to prevent falls. I propose that guard rail be built of the same sandstone as the facing and wrapped completely around the tower. That way, it will become a part of the design and not detract from the overall look.

"Using the average floor to ceiling height for rooms in both private dwellings and office space of nine feet, that means approximately 9 feet, 6 inches per level, taking into consideration the height needed for the framing between floors. Using those parameters, I have made the towers twenty floors tall, or approximately 200 feet. This is well within the height limit of buildings near airports.

"Gordan, when we first started talking about these towers, you asked if they would be connected in any way. In these plans, you will notice I have shown them over a full first floor basement service area. When I say FULL basement, I mean just that. This shows a complete concreted floor under all towers and then connecting tunnels under the roadways. The roads will need to have some supports, but the tunnels will be used to get from one tower to another, or out to the rest of the Resort. Even the area right under each tower will be put to good use for parking cars, or docking bays for deliveries, and laundry or trash collection sections. I'm sure Russell will come up with more ideas.

"Also, one last thing. To stabilize these tall structures in case of high winds coming in from the river, or even as far away as the Gulf at times, I have put in a crosswalk close to the top of the towers to connect all four. This crosswalk will meet in the center, directly over the grassy strip between the four-lane highway. A supporting structure will have to be put in there from the bottom of the connecting point to the ground. Even better, down into the basement area for a good foundation. This could be much like those poles we see holding up very large billboards along some roads. This will not only support the crosswalk but will also help stabilize the whole complex if those high winds the Gulf is known for come ashore here. Hurricanes have been known to reach even as far as Bob's ranch, and I want to plan ahead.

"Well, gentlemen, what do you think?"

Silence.

Finally, Bill said "I need to get in touch with the roadbuilding company again. I never had these things come up when they built the roads out to the oil fields. However, I think they would be the best people to tunnel under the roads and put in the necessary supports. They already know what they are dealing with. But where will we put all that dirt?"

"Most of it can be used to build up the airstrip. Where we planned to put it happens to be in the lowest section of the Resort. We would need to bring in dirt anyway or see the landing strip flooded often."

Gordan said "I am getting rather excited about these towers of yours, King, and the whole Resort idea is sounding better and better as the new areas are beginning to be developed, however there is one thing we really haven't addressed. What are we going to call our new Resort? It can't continue to be "The Site" forever."

"Funny you should mention that just now." King said. "While I was playing around with the plans at home this past week, Abbie came in and saw what I was doing. She said, and I quote, 'Oh, you are working on the Clover Leaf Towers.' It hit me then that we could call them just that, as we were planning to name all the Villages anyway. The towers will be one of our Villages, as well as a landmark in the whole area. What would you think of naming the entire project Clover Leaf Resort? It just might bring us Good Luck!"

Again, complete silence.

Bill was the first to speak, and said he approved.

Gordan soon agreed, and they called in Kelly to tell her to start ordering all the stationary for the office with that name on it, and a large four-leaf clover should be the logo for the entire Resort.

"We have accomplished a great deal here this morning, but most of it was from my tower plans. What have you two been up to? Bill, I know you have been out of town, but things were getting done before that. What new projects are being worked on?"

"I have called on my friends with the state department that deal with putting in hiking trails in our state parks. While we will not be under their jurisdiction, they gave me some contacts. One of them, a Mr. Levy, will be here to meet with me tomorrow. Gordan and I also are getting the roads in the rest of this village completed. That should be completed within the month, and we can start building more of these Duplex units. I guess we will have to come up with another name!"

Gordan spoke up to say "Along with the roads in this village, we need to take another look at the map to settle on where the other villages will be. With that settled, the roads can be put in while the crews are here and that will save us some money. The utilities can go in at the same time, which will also save a little money. These contractors don't like to make multiple trips this far out. The more we can have them do while they are working here, the cheaper the charges are. When will you be ready for the utilities in the towers, King?"

"Russell and I have a conference call scheduled for this evening to discuss how he is coming along with the interior designs. I should know about utilities after that."

"Great!

"I have made good progress with the company that will be building the fishing pier and boat house. They even gave me the name of a company that could supply all the paddle boats we would need, plus a few regular row boats. Another thought came to me while I was talking to them. I believe we should think about putting in a small lake that could be stocked with trout or other fish. Not all our guests are going to like the catfish in the river. I admit, most of them do taste of the mud they live in."

"We can look at a good place for that when we check out the new village sites. That can be tomorrow, right"

"Suits me." Bill said. "Now, can we go outside and talk a minute?"

Once outside and moved away from the office several yards, he continued. "I have a suggestion about the name of this village if you two agree. I think we should call it 'Kelly Place'. Our Kelly has worked hard for us, sometimes under trying and lonely conditions, and even cooking for us often. I'd like to show her our appreciation."

"What a fantastic idea, Bill!" Gordan said.

"I like it." King added. "Do you want to go in and tell her now?"

"No. I think something this special should be done over a celebratory meal. I'll order in a good lunch for the day after tomorrow. Will that work for you two?"

"Super! Now I'm going home to get my papers together for when Russell calls. See you tomorrow."

Russell called right on time and started talking as soon as King came on the line. "Sam wanted me to tell you that Si has finished the foundation for her house using the suggestions you gave him. He expects to start with the framing next week. She and Jeff are getting so excited about maybe moving in before their baby is born."

"Well, that's good news. How is your other crew doing with that grocery store you are putting up in the village?"

"All going well, and since it's almost finished, I have been able to put a lot of time on these plans for your towers. Once I figured out the best way to make it work, the plans came together quickly. Even better, with a few minor changes, the same plans can be used for all four towers!"

"That sounds terrific! Tell me more."

"O.K. basically, your towers will be very large circles, right? Well, Granny Edi brought one of her peach pies into the family room so Katie could cut it for us, and I could only visualize that pie as one of your towers. You know how Granny always has a hole in the middle of the top crust to let out the steam? Well, that 'steam hole' in the middle of your towers becomes the elevator shaft, with all the utility pipes and cables in it for all the floors, just like you have in The Castle. Now, all the way around the elevator shaft except where the doors open, we add heavy acrylic walls for a light well like the one I put in my home, except it would be much taller. Then, add to that wall the width of a wide corridor all the way around, and you have a hallway for the tenants, lit by some daylight and with LED bulbs behind the acrylic. Now, on the other side of that hallway, you cut 'pie slices' out to the outside walls of the tower. To the crust of the pie if you like. Those slices can then be divided into various rooms for each apartment. Use two slices or even more for a larger apartment, or even a shop for the commercial tower or a business office or classroom if you go with the idea of adding a complete school in one of the towers. What do you think, so far?"

"I like the concept a lot. Using the same basic design will save a lot of building time. Now, have you thought about the ground floor? The other guys want to know about utilities so we can get them all done at the same time."

"Well, yea, we can use the same layout. All the utilities would be inside the elevator shaft, and it would just be a matter of connecting them to the main lines for the Resort. As for the 'pie slices' they could be used for the laundry room, housekeeping, security, heating, and air conditioning equipment, whatever is needed for the upkeep of each tower. I think I can design trash drops on each floor for trash, recyclables, and maybe even laundry chutes to make the housekeeping job easier, then put large collection bins on the ground floor. There may be other details that will come up later, but that is about all I have right now. Are you going to need to add more crews to build all the new projects going on at once?"

"Yes, at least two more crews, I think. Unemployment is high in this area right new, so it shouldn't be hard. When can you come out to see what's going on?"

"I could probably get away for a few days next week if you could use the jet to cut down on the time involved. Why don't you and Abbie come for an overnight? I know she is not going to want to fly much longer, and Granny Edi would love to see her."

"Good idea. I'll call later to set it up."

"Super! I may even 'treat' Katie to a vacation at a fashionable Resort for a few days! Does that one unit already finished come equipped with a crib?"

"I'll make sure that it has one by the time Susan gets here. And speaking of cribs, I gotta' go help get our babies ready for bed. Talk to you soon. Bye."

Chapter Twenty

A s soon as King got into the office in the Kelly Place village the next day, he told the other two the plans Russell had talked about. They both liked what they heard and told King to push forward in getting Clover Leaf Towers up as soon as possible. King then asked Kelly to put an ad in the paper for construction workers and asked her to order one dozen baby cribs to be put in the rental units as needed.

Bill, Gordan, and King then settled down to go over the maps to plan the villages and pond. During that discussion, Gordan suggested that they purchase a few golf cart-like vehicles for the employees to use while traveling around the Resort.

"It would be a good idea if we took a closer look at some of these places, but the ones way out at the borders are just too far to walk to in this heat, especially that one we are thinking about putting on top of the high hill."

"Kelly, how about ordering six of those things and have them bill me directly. I can then take one up to my largest oil field and inspect it in more comfort. Now, I have to go meet with Mr. Levy about those trails."

"And since I can't do anything more on the towers or this village until I have more construction workers, I'm going home to start the drawings for the stable. Gordan, the place is all yours for the rest of the day."

Abbie could not fly East with him to pick up Russell and Katie because she had a doctor's appointment but said she would go with him when he carried them back. Therefore, it was a quick turnaround trip with King not even going out to the house. Jeff brought the Mayhew family to the airport, they loaded the luggage, and headed back to Texas. When King drove them out to the resort the next day, Russell was impressed with what had been accomplished since he had been there. Katie was happy to meet Gordan and complemented him on his idea to turn his property into something a lot of people would enjoy. The other half of the Duplex met with her approval, and she even had a few suggestions for improving the next ones to be built.

King offered to drive her out to see the stable area while Bill and Gordan brought Russell up on what was going on. Katie jumped at the chance and followed her brother out to his car. After strapping Susan in, they headed toward a large barn going up out close to the air strip, but far enough away from it that the planes would not bother the horses.

"Are you guys furnishing all the horses, or do you expect most of them will be owned by the guests?"

"Well, at least a few of them will be privately owned, but I want to check out rescue stables like Abbie's friend Mr. O'Shay owns. Also, Bob has offered one or two from the ranch. He has a couple that are getting a little old for the ranch work but would do well here for the 'unschooled rider' that will not demand too much from their mount. Finding competent stable help should not prove to be much of a problem. This is horse country after all. And of course, 'Mr. Saddles' himself is providing all the tack we will need."

"Wonderful! Now, I think we need to return to Kelly Place so Little Miss Susan here can have a nap."

Kelly had made a wonderful dinner for all of them, and while talking afterward, Katie found out she had gone to high school with Kelly's Mom. There was a lot of catching up to do, and that discussion carried over into the next day, when Katie was not being shown around the Resort. Russell was ready to go home the following morning to work on some new ideas for the towers, so the Mayhew family and the Coles left early the next day to head East. King had told his partners not to expect him back for three or four days, as he wanted some time to visit with the rest of his family.

They made good time and Sam picked them up at the airport. Everyone back at the house gave them a big welcome, and the first thing King did was ask Granny Edi for a piece of her pie. She got a kick out of the story about her pie giving Russell the inspiration for King's towers. Doc had come in from his clinic at the Retirement Home, so it was a wonderful family reunion.

The next day, Sam and Jeff took King and Abbie to show off how much Si had finished on their new house. There was a great deal to show off, as Sam had been pushing Si to work his crew hard. She really wanted to be in her new house when the baby was born.

Back in the living room, they were enjoying their after-dinner drinks when Jeff's phone buzzed. "Oh, I hope it's not an emergency! I really don't want to go back in tonight. Hello, this is Dr. Jef…"

"Yes, yes, I know who you are, and I have a lot to say to you in a short amount of time. I am Trever Lewis, the attorney handling Miss Carolyn Conklin's estate. I will have to meet you tomorrow to get the paperwork signed, but I just wanted to let you know, she has left her entire estate to you and your hospital, but she wants it used to build a new children's wing at the hospital. It is a very large sum of money, and needs to be handled carefully, so there will be a lot of paperwork involved. I will meet you in your office at ten o'clock tomorrow. Good evening."

Jeff pulled the phone away from his ear and just stared at it.

"Jeff? Jeff, are you all right?" Sam asked him.

"No. Yes. Maybe. I don't know! That was the strangest call I have ever gotten except the one telling me Abbie had disappeared."

He took a deep breath, then told the family what had occurred.

"Oh, Carolyn! I didn't know she was gone." Granny Edi told them.

"So, you knew her?"

"Oh, yes. She was a member of my group back in the day. That was so long ago! We were a close-knit group back then, about ten or twelve of us. Then some went away to college, some went into the military, some got married right out of high school and moved away. The group never was as close again, and I lost touch with most of them over the years. I heard from Molly that Carolyn went to college, fell in love with a boy she met there, and was planning a big wedding to be held in that beautiful mansion on the hill above the hospital. One week before the wedding, she got word that he had married someone else.

"She became a recluse after that and was never seen in the village again. She hired a widow to become her companion, and they lived alone with only a few servants to care for her and the estate. She always sent large quantities of handmade items to be sold at our church charity events, but never came to any of them. I have also heard that she was very well off, thanks to some wise investments her father had made, and she continued with them after his death. That may be a sizeable gift she has left you, Jeff."

"Well, I guess I'll find out tomorrow. Too bad the lawyer was such a gruff sort. I would like to have asked him some question. Maybe I'll get a chance to learn more tomorrow."

He did get a chance and had to reverse his opinion of the lawyer.

When his secretary showed Mr. Trever Lewis into the office the next day, Jeff was shocked at his look of confusion and sadness. He soon found out why he looked that way.

"I'm sorry I was so abrupt last evening, Doctor, but it was a bad time for me. You see, my mother was the companion for Miss Carolyn for many years. I was one week old when my father walked out, leaving Mother with little money and a newborn child to support. She was very happy to find a job where she could keep me with her. I grew up there and we both loved Miss Carolyn deeply. Not many people even knew I existed for years, as I was happy to play in the back yard and stay out of sight if anyone came to the house. My only friend was a boy who lived a block away, but we were good buddies.

Still are. I was tutored for years by those two ladies, then sent to a private school out of state. They did not mean for my presence to be a big secret; they just didn't see that it was anyone's business. They never tried to hide me. I was always encouraged to speak to the mailman or whoever delivered the newspaper or groceries, but both were very private people and tried to keep their lives as private as possible.

"Anyway, when I graduated from college, I went to Law School, and now have been handling Miss Carolyn's affairs for years. As well as my mothers. She followed Miss Carolyn's example and invested her income wisely. If you need to check me out, here is my card. As you can see, my office in the old section of the next town and I do mostly pro bono work. Thanks to my mother and an allowance from Miss Carolyn for many years, and some good investments of my own, I do well. My wife also has a good job, so we don't need anything more. I'm telling you all of this, so you understand. ALL of Miss Carolyn's estate, **everything**, has been left to your hospital. I get nothing, which is the way I wanted it. Mother would not have received anything either. Unfortunately, the shock of having Miss Carolyn die in her arms two nights ago distressed Mother so, she had a massive heart attack early yesterday and died before the servants could even call for help. So, you see why I was not in a very talkative mood last night when I called you. I would not have called so soon, but that directive was in Miss Carolyn's will also."

"Saints preserve us, what a story! So, what do we do now?"

"I just need you to sign these papers accepting the responsibility of the money in the name of the hospital and promising to start a new wing within one year. That's it. I'll give you a certified check in the amount of the monetary value of the full estate and the deed to the house, and we are finished."

Chapter Twenty-one

J EFF WAS STILL PRETTY much shell-shocked when he arrived home that evening. He had just sat at his desk for several minutes after Mr. Lewis had gone, just staring at the check. He found it extremely hard to realize that much money had just been handed to him. He finally got up, grabbed the check, and practically ran to the bookkeeper's office. He told her to set up a separate account for the new wing, and to call a board meeting so he could advise them about what had happened. Then he left for home.

He was gratified to see he wasn't the only one shocked at the amount of the check. Granny Edi just barely stopped herself from saying 'I told you so!', and the others were very happy for the hospital.

"Now comes the hard part." Jeff said to them. "I'm going to have to hire a manager to deal with getting the new wing built. I can't take that much time from my practice and running the hospital."

Sam spoke up to say "Why do you need to hire someone when a perfectly capable manager is sitting right here? I would love to tackle that job, and my experience dealing with the company that re-did the waiting areas should come in handy."

"Now, Sam, be careful what you sign up for." Katie said. "Aren't you supposed to be resting a lot?"

"Ah, but most of the work is already done! Russell's third work crew is just about finished with the new grocery store, and I will, of course, hire Mayhew and Cole Construction, Inc. to do the whole project. The hard decision will be to come up with a plan about the wonderful old house."

Katie turned to Russell and said "Have you completed all you have to do for the Clover Leaf Resort? Will you have time to take on a hospital wing?"

"I still have a few more details to iron out with the towers, but after that, King can pretty much handle everything else. Right, Bro?"

"Pretty much. I'm working on the stable right now and will start on the hanger for the air strip after that. Both of those will be simple rectangles, so I think I can handle it!"

"Ha, ha! But you know Gordan said he didn't want anything too simple, so add a few corners or a high-pitched roof or two to keep him happy."

"Talking about new hospital wings and what you are planning for your Resort got me to wondering." Granny Edi was always interested in what 'her grandchildren' were doing, and sometimes offered good advice. Such as now. "With all those people coming out there to have fun and play hard, and some even living there all year, I hope you are planning a clinic on the property. Much like you put out at the rest home."

"And yet another thing to add to a tower! But thank you, Granny Edi. We will need at least a First Aid Station. I'm glad you brought it up. Oh, adding to the towers reminded me. Katie, Bill spoke to Megan several days age and she is interested in expanding her restaurant business to the resort. She says if we will let her rent the whole top floor of the Business Office Tower, she will open "One Step Up" as soon as possible."

Will said "I just love it when all these people come together to work on one project. You aren't by any chance selling shares in this Resort Complex, are you? I think Meli and I might like to become a part of that."

"Hey! What a fantastic idea. Sam and I just might like to have a few shares also."

Russell said "That subject has never come up, but it just might be something Gordan would consider. It would help cover the cost of all the amenities he wants to put in. We can run it by him and put it to a vote. That sounds rather weird. The four of us act as if it is a cooperation already, but there is no chairman. We just seem to agree on whatever comes up. It is still Gordan's property, so we tend to listen when he speaks, but he listens to our ideas too."

"Sounds like we need to have a meeting pretty soon. Do you want to fly back out with me, or do it with a Conference Call?"

"Definitely a Conference Call. It looks like I will be tied up here planning a hospital wing! Thank goodness, they all need to be standard layouts, so it won't be too difficult, but I do need to be here to supervise for most it. It least until Si gets through with Sam's house. Then he can take over both crews and get it done quicker."

Abbie had been whispering with Sam while they were talking, and then said to King "Dear, handsome, sweet, wonderful husband, Sam and I would like to ask a question."

"Watch out, Bro! With an intro like that, it's gotta' be big."

This was repeated in some form all around the room.

"Well, not too big I hope." Abbie said. "Megan wanting to expand gave me the idea. What if one of those shops in the business tower was a sewing shop? It would give another outlet for Sam's and my fabrics."

"Whew! I thought you were going to throw something at me I couldn't do. That will be easy. You should probably visit Pins 'N Needles here in town tomorrow and see how she set up her business. It helps to get all the information you can before you start something like this."

"As long as you are going in, anyway, please bring me more yarn. I have two more baby sweaters to knit!" Granny was very happy about the expected additions to the family and had already finished knitting blankets for each.

The ladies began what sounded like it was going to be a very long discussion on baby colors, what else the new mothers might need, and several other subjects. Russell silently stood and motioned to the other guys, giving them clues with his hands to follow him downstairs to the billiards table. They quickly got up to follow him. The ladies barely knew when they left.

The next two days were spent in much the same manor, with lots of joking around, and teasing, and sharing stories of their day. Abbie, King, and their twins left to go back to Texas. Sam visited her new house site daily and worked on plans for the new children's wing. On evening when Doc Simmons came by to visit, they were talking about just that.

"You know, Sam, I may have a suggestion for you about the mansion right above the hospital. I was chatting with one of the residents last week, and she was telling me about a friend of hers whose daughter had a child in a hospital out west somewhere. I think it was out west. Whatever. Anyway, she said the parents were able to stay in a little hotel the hospital owned just for that purpose. It was right next door to the hospital; the parents could live there free while the child was a patient and take turns visiting with their child whenever they wanted to. They even had access to laundry facilities and a kitchen. That house of Carolyn's would do very well as a parent's retreat."

"Oh, what a splendid idea, Doc. I'll investigate setting up a fundraising event to help with the upkeep, and maybe even find a business that would be interested in sponsoring the project. At least enough to pay a cleaning staff. Thank you!"

As it happened, Mr. Trever Lewis heard of the plans and called Sam one evening.

"Trever Lewis here. Good evening, Mrs. Barlow. I hope I am not calling at a bad time, but there is something I would like to discuss with you."

"This is a perfect time, Mr. Lewis. What is it?"

"I heard about what you have in mind for Miss Carolyn's home, and I want to help. You see, those investments Miss Carolyn had were included in her estate. They were all covered in the money I gave to your husband. However, the ones my mother had passed to me at her death. I would like to sign those investments over to set up a trust to take care of the house pretty much forever. If you do not dip too heavily into the principle, the interest should be enough to support the house and a couple of servants for many, many years. As a matter of fact, the cook and housekeeper are still living there until they can find a new job. That was also spelled out in the will. I believe they might be convinced to stay on."

"Oh! Mr. Lewis! This is wonderful. May I go and talk to them tomorrow?"

"Of course. As a matter of fact, why don't I meet you there? Cora and Hazel used to spank me regularly, after I had swiped one too many cookies or slid down the bannister one too many times. I'm sure they would like to see me all grown up!"

"Great! Would nine thirty be too early for you?"

"That would be fine. I'll see you tomorrow."

Both were right on time and as they walked up to the front door, it flew open to allow a tall thin woman to come racing down to meet them.

Oh, Mr. Trev! It's so quiet here without your dear Mamma and Miss Carolyn. Can't you come back to live here?"

"Ah, Cora, you know that isn't possible. I explained all this just after Mother's funeral."

"She just doesn't want to hear it, nor do I." This came from a completely opposite lady, physically speaking. Rather stout, and very short, this lady also had an apron tied around her waist, but that was the only thing in common as far as Sam could tell.

"Hazel, you still smell like cinnamon!" Trever said as he picked her up and spun her around, then did the same with Cora.

"Put me down, you prankster! Still joking around, I see. Didn't that fancy school teach you anything?"

"Nothing has changed since I saw you last week, Scarecrow. Except, the reason I brought this lady to see you today. Can we go inside, or do we have to talk on the front porch? And yes, I know "Wipe your feet, young man!""

Settled in the front parlor with a cup of tea in her hands, Sam couldn't help but look around at the beautiful room.

"This is the only room in the whole house I was not allowed to enter except on special occasions. Miss Carolyn insisted I be married in here, right over there in front of the fireplace. I think she was re-living her own plans, but she didn't say anything about that. Just welcomed Irene into the family and gave us a wonderful reception. Small by most standards, but wonderful all the same." Turning to the two ladies standing in the doorway, he said "Now, we should probably get down to the reason we are here and asked the two of you to stay." He began to tell them about the plans for the house but was interrupted by Cora.

"We know all about the plans, Mr. Trev. The mailman told us and then Clarence when he delivered the groceries said it was so. I think Miss Carolyn would approve of you saving her house this way, but Hazel and I are going to say 'No' to your plans for us. And, yes, we figured out you would want us to stay here. You are just that much like your Mamma. But we are just too old. We helped raise you, so that makes us ancient!

"Actually, we are going out to the lake and get a two-bedroom apartment at Bradley Place. Some of our friends are already there, and I understand you know the two fellows that re-built it. Nice guys, I hear. But anyway, we have already found our replacements for here, so you don't have to worry about that Mrs. Barlow. My niece and her two grown children can move in the first of next week, just after we leave for the lake, and they will take very good care of this wonderful house. They will all work for the same salary you would pay Hazel and me. The son is a good handyman, the girl is a good housekeeper, and my niece is an excellent cook. I think you will be pleased with them."

"Well, it looks like I didn't need to be here at all! Thank you so much for getting a replacement staff. There is one question. What's to happen with all this gorgeous furniture? Mr. Lewis, you grew up with these pieces. Surely you would like to claim something?"

"All of this now belongs to the hospital board, however there are one or two pieces I wouldn't mind having. I'll ask if I can be at the next meeting."

"I'm sure Jeff would welcome you. Call him soon, though. I understand that meeting is soon."

Chapter Twenty-two

THE HOSPITAL GAVE MR. Lewis and the two servants permission to take anything out of the house they wanted. Cora and Hazel accepted gladly the furniture from their old rooms to move to their new apartment. Trever Lewis asked for the small writing desk that had been in the sitting room and his mother's favorite rocking chair. All the clothing for both ladies went to charity.

The process for the new wing went smoothly and they were ready to accept patients much sooner than expected. Two of those patients lived in the next state, so their parents lived in the "Carolyn House" and gave it good marks on the review form.

Sam was glad when the new wing was finished so she could rest. She hadn't realized how much time had been needed for the project but was glad to be a part of it. There was a great sense of pride in a job well done.

They were all in the living room one evening when Katie's phone rang. At the completion of the call, she told the others "That was Mr. Jacob Finnigan. He wanted to let me know he was leaving this weekend for that conference he told us about. He is still taking two of my dogs and has scheduled two separate classes to show off what they can do. I hope they don't embarrass him. OR me! This could be very good advertising for Katie's Kennels, or I may never sell another dog to the State Police. I will be very interested to see what this conference brings."

About a week later, out in Texas, King was just getting home from a long day out at Clover Leaf Resort. They had voted to open to investors and were now "a real cooperation with a board and everything" as Kelly said. Gordan was, of course, Chairman of the Board, Bill was CEO, and Russell and King happy to be just members, but now with shares in the company. A residential tower had been finished and an office tower and a mall started. Leaving the fourth tower until they got state approval, they planned to make it an educational building. It would contain a lower school, high school, and community college, plus a large public library on the first floor. The towers were well on their way to becoming the 'small city' Gordan had talked about.

King walked into the living room, dropped his briefcase on the floor, then followed it down so he could tickle Ren. Rona was already being played with by Maria, while Abbie smiled at them all from her rocking chair. When the house phone rang, Maria jumped up to answer it. She came back to tell King "There is a Mister Jacob Finnigan on the line. He says he knows our Katie and would like to speak to you."

King jumped up, grabbed the handset and said "What's wrong? Is Katie alright?"

"She's fine. At least when I left the East, she was. I didn't mean to frighten you, but was sure you didn't remember me, and I felt I needed to talk to you. This is really none of my business, but I have gotten to know the family well since I purchased a couple of Katie's pups a couple of years ago. I have two of them here with me at the State Police Convention. I was wondering if you could please meet me here for lunch tomorrow? We will be at One Hundred and One for the demonstration, and I would like to see you there. It starts at eleven and should be over about twelve. There is someone I would like you to meet, and he will be helping with the demonstration, so if you could be here just before eleven, that would be great. I'd like you to see him before I introduce him to you. I know all of this is very mysterious, but there is a reason I am being so secretive. Trust me, if my gut feeling isn't wrong, and it seldom is, you will be glad you came. It may concern Samantha as well. Will I see you tomorrow?"

"With an exit line like that, you bet I'll be there! Can you tell me anything more?"

"No. I don't want you to prejudge anything. Bring Abbie too if she feels up to it. Another set of eyes might be helpful. Good night, Sleep well!"

King would have had to tie Abbie to her chair to keep her from going with him the next day. They arrived fifteen minutes early, gave Megan a hug, and asked where the dog demonstration was to be held. Going quietly into the Ballroom, they took seats off to one side of the stage. One of the hosting troopers gave a short welcoming speech, then introduced Mr. Jacob Finnigan and his dogs. Jacob took one dog through his paces, then said "To help me with the next dog, I have a fellow trooper up here with me. I'd like to introduce Matthew Robert Jenkins. Matthew is a State Trooper from way up in Alaska. I mean WAY up, almost to the end of the world! Matt, will you please bring out Ginger? A tall young man in his full State trooper dress uniform came further on stage, leading a beautiful golden retriever with him. Jacob and Matt asked her to perform some very difficult "finds", and she did all of them very well. All eyes were on the dog except King's. Because of what this Mr. Finnigan had told him, he was watching Matt Jenkins closely. He also noticed Abbie was more interested in the young man then she was the demonstration.

After the dogs had left the stage, and the audience began leaving, Abbie turned to King and said "Why do I feel I have met that young man before? I don't think I know any Jenkins."

King just shook his head and said, "Let's go find Mr. Finnigan and maybe he can clear this up."

As it happened, Megan met them just as they came out the door and said, "Please follow me". She led them first to the elevators, then showed them to one of the private rooms on the fourth floor, all without saying anything else. When they went inside, Mr. Finnigan came over to shake hands, then turned and introduced them to Matt. Just then, waiters came in and served them a delicious looking meal, so they all sat down.

Mr. Finnigan said "In order to save time, I took the liberty of ordering for us. If you would rather have something else just nod to one of the waiters. Matt, I purchased those two dogs you have been working with from King's sister. I have since become friends with the rest of that rather unusual family. The reason I'm telling you this is so that you will feel comfortable when I ask you to repeat to them the story you shared with me."

"Oh, but you are not a stranger. These people will think I'm crazy."

"I assure you they will think no such thing! Go on, start at the beginning."

"Well, if you say so." He took a deep breath then began. "For a very long time now, years, I have felt I'm not who I've been told I am. And I was right! I just learned the truth from my aunt two years ago as she was dying. She said she just couldn't keep the secret any longer and wanted me to know. It seems she was not my aunt at all but the sister of the woman I always thought of as my mother. It seems that was not true either. Aunt Gail told me that her sister, Betty, married very young, moved to the Lower States, had a son, and was very happy. Then both her husband and son were killed in an automobile accident. Her husband was a low-ranking man in service, so she didn't have a lot of money when he died. She went to work for a couple as a caregiver for their children while they were at work in their Real Estate office. Then, one day, as she was walking their son to his nursery school two blocks away, she just kept going and never looked back. I nev..."

"WAIT! I know this story!" Abbie had jumped up from her chair and was staring at Matt. "That woman dyed your hair, changed your clothes, changed your name, and just kept on doing that over and over and kept going from one place to another until the FBI lost the trail. They searched for you for three years, gathering little bits of information until they ran out of anyone who had seen her and you. My God! You're Tommy, Sam's brother! She thought you were dead!"

She collapsed into her seat, and King grabbed her to hold her close. "Are you sure, Abbie?"

"Yes, I'm positive. Back when I first came to Melrose Farm, Sam and I were very close. We would talk and talk about things that had gone on in our lives before we met there. Sometimes she would get very teary and tell me all she could remember about the brother she adored but lost. What he just said is the same story she told me. Not the part about his aunt, of course but the rest of it is almost word for word what she told me.

"I knew it!" Mr. Finnigan almost shouted.

Matt just sat with a bewildered look on his face, then whispered "I've found my sister! She was real all this time! I thought I just dreamed her up to keep me company."

"King, you simply must take him to Melrose Farm as quickly as the jet can get you there! This is unbelievable!"

King turned to Mr. Finnigan and said "How soon can you and, Umm? Matt get checked out of your hotel and be ready to head East?"

"As this is the last day of the conference, we both checked out before we came here. But I do have my dogs."

"With crates?" King asked.

"Naturally"

"Then there is no problem. We can strap them down in the plane. Come on, Abbie can drop us off at the airport on her way home. NO! Abbie, you cannot go. You are too close to your due date. It isn't safe for you."

"I know, I know. I would just like to see Sam's face when she realizes Robbie is right there! Once you are airborne, I'm going to call Katie and tell her what has happened. She should get the family together to support Sam when she hears. She is almost as close to her due date as I am."

"You mean I'm going to be an uncle? I have a real family? Yes, this is truly unbelievable."

Chapter Twenty-three

WHEN KATIE FINISHED HER phone call with Abbie, she just sat with a shocked look on her face. Russell came over to her chair and put his arm around her. "What's up, Love. I heard you say Abbie, but then nothing much else, except 'I'll take care of it'. Take care of what?"

"Sit down, Russell. You are not going to believe this. And we must figure out how to protect Sam. Can you call Jeff and ask him to come over? And maybe Meli too. What about Granny Edi. Wait. I'm rambling. This is just such a shock. O.K. Yes, that was Abbie calling to let us know King is in the air right now, headed here with Mr. Finnigan, his dogs, and SAM'S LONG-LOST BROTHER!"

"What!"

"You heard correctly. It seems Mr. Finnigan met a young man at his conference that reminded him so much of our Sam, he called King to come met him to see if he got the same feeling. Abbie went with King, heard only a part of this young man's story, and remembered Sam telling her the same story about losing her brother. They immediately went to the airport and are on their way here now. We must get the family together, but I wouldn't want to tell Sam and get her all excited if it turns out this man is not her brother. I think we need to tell Jeff, and maybe even call Doc just in case. You know she is very near her due date. If it's true, news like this could send her into labor."

"I'll call Jeff right away. After we tell him what's about to happen, we'll let him decide how to break this to Sam."

Jeff came running into Katie's kitchen. "What's wrong? You said it was urgent, and for me to bring Meli and Will. What is going on?"

"Well, it is in a way, but nothing is wrong." Katie got up and poured a cup of coffee for him, refilled hers and Russell's, then sat back down. "At least, I don't think so. I thought Meli and Will would come over with you."

I'm sure they would have, but neither one is home right now. Meli has gone with Sam to take Cisco and Charlie to the Vet for their annual shots, and Will went to pick up something he left in his office at the University. Is this something they need to know?"

"Yes, but you can tell them later, but we do need your help with something concerning Sam."

"Sam!" he asked. "What help does she need?"

After Katie explained what Abbie had told her, Jeff was as shocked as any of them. He knew about Sam's brother, but thought, as she did, that after all this time, he would either have been found or had died.

"I think the best thing for Sam's health is to NOT tell her this man is, or may be, her brother. Let him come in, be introduced, and see how she reacts. If he is Tommie, we will have a joyful reunion. If he isn't, she will not be upset. How soon should we expect them, Russell?"

"I'd give them another two hours at least. I'll run out to the airport in plenty of time. You and Katie figure out how you're going to get everyone together without letting the cat out of the bag."

"I know what we can do." Jeff said a few minutes later. "You said Mr. Finnigan is with them? That's the perfect excuse! We can say he would like to come by and tell Katie how the dogs performed, and she would like the whole family to hear it too."

"Perfect! I really do want to find out how the dogs did, but this other news made that so much less important."

Sam and Meli each took an animal carrier into the vet's office and laughed at the children leaving their own pets to come and play with the monkey. Cisco was happy to show off for them and waved Goodbye to each as they took their pet into the back. They were finally called in, both animals given a good report, and got back into Meli's car.

"Don't forget to run by the furniture store so I can check on the new things. They are supposed to be here by the end of the week. I'm hoping it will be sooner so they can be delivered before Jeff and I move into the house."

"How much does Si have to finish? Russell thought he had about completed the job."

"Not a lot, really, just some trim work in all but our bedroom. But that must be installed, sanded, and painted. Jeff refuses to let me stay in the house more than five minutes while there is even a whiff of paint odor, so I am behind in what I wanted to have done by now. But my favorite doctor tells me to stop running my blood pressure up by stressing so much. He says I will have plenty of time to do all that even after the baby comes. I know he is correct, but I still want it done NOW!"

"And you have been that way ever since I've known you, he is right. I'm sure your new Dining Room set will be here soon, so don't worry so much. That can't be good for you or the baby."

"Now you are sounding just like Jeff" Wow, were you expecting company?"

"No, but that looks like Mr. Finnigan's car, so it is probably something to do with Katie's dogs. Or rather, his dogs now. You do know he took them out to give a demonstration at the convention? Looks like he is back."

An hour later, everyone was sitting around in the living room eating pie and drinking coffee. Mr. Finnigan played his role to the hilt, telling them about how well the dogs behaved, all the time watching Sam watching Matt and Matt watching Sam. As the plates were being collected, Matt couldn't wait any longer. He went over to Sam, stood right in front of her and said "Hi, SammyAnn."

She gasped, struggled to her feet, and said, "Take off your shirt and turn around!"

There were shocked reactions all around the room, with Granny Edi saying "Samantha! Where are your manners?"

Matt just gave them all a big smile, lifted his hand to stop the questions and turned around as he was unbuttoning his uniform jacket. He folded it neatly and dropped it over the arm of his chair, then unbuttoned his dress shirt, folding it as neatly, and placed it on top of his jacket, then pulled his undershirt over his head and, very slowly folding it as neatly, dropped it too. Then he leaned over to put his shoulder into

Sam's vision. On the back of his left shoulder was a dark birthmark in the shape of a small sickle.

Sam almost collapsed and would have if Jeff hadn't been standing right beside her. She was whispering "Tommysickle!" over and over. Then "It can't be you. But it is! Oh, Tommy, where have you been all these years?"

Once all the hugging and hand shaking had slowed down, Matt was asked to tell them his story.

"The woman who took me had a sister who was a teacher on the very last inhabited island in the Aleutian chain. It is almost out to Attu Island and that is the last island belonging to the U.S." Grinning at Mr. Finnigan, he added "When this gentleman said I was from the end of the world, he was close. Anyway, I grew up living with the family until I graduated from high school, then I moved to Anchorage and put myself through college, then on to the State Police Academy there.

"I asked for and was given the area of my hometown as the place to patrol and worked there until Aunt Gail told me this story. All this time, I believed the woman I called Mother really was my mother, but I kept remembering living somewhere else, and calling some other woman 'Mom'. I also remembered someone I called SammyAnn, but then would think that couldn't be so. I was an only child, so could not have a sister. But it kept bugging me. When Aunt Gail died, I felt there was nothing to hold me in that little place anymore and figured I could probably find out the truth about my real family easier if I lived in the Lower Forty-eight. I have been searching for you for six years, SammyAnn. Now I know who I really am!"

"You are Thomas Robert Matthews, Jr. and you did call our mother 'Mom'. She was devastated when you disappeared. You were only four years old, and she felt guilty because she went back to work so soon after your birth. She died of a broken heart about four years later, right after the FBI told us they were closing the case. Daddy followed her six months later."

Matt lowered his head to his hands for a few minutes, then said "I am so sorry I caused all that grief. It was certainly not intentional! Come to think of it, I believe it was about four years after I came to live with the Jenkins family that I started having the dreams about a mom and a sister. But a father figure never appeared in those nightmares. I wonder why?"

"Daddy loved you very much, but worked long hours at his office, always taking around clients to show houses and such. When he finally came home, he was too tired to play with us much. He tried to make up for it on weekends, but it was never enough for either of us. I missed him too. He was never there to admire my new dress, or help with my homework, or any of the other things girls and their Daddies do together. And let that be a lesson to you Jeff! If we have a girl, I will expect you to be attentive."

"Yes, Mam! And to show you how attentive I can be, I'm going remind you that it's time for your nap. You've had a shock today, so it's even more important for you to rest. I'm sure your brother will still be here when you get up."

"I will be around for as long as she will put up with me. Now that we have found each other, I don't want to go away any time soon!"

Sam said "Just one more question before I go. However did you find him, King?"

"Not me! That was Mr. Finnigan."

"Mr. Finnigan? But how did you know? I mean, what made you connect the two of us?"

"My dear, you have been a puzzle to me ever since the first day I met you! I think I may have even embarrassed you at times when I kept looking at you. You reminded me of someone, but I just could never remember where I had seen whoever it was. Then, this last time at the convention, this young fellow volunteered to help me show off the dogs. We had met at conventions for several years, but never got close. Now we worked together often, and one day after working with the dogs, we went for a cup of coffee. He felt comfortable enough with me by then to share a story about how he was searching for his sister without even knowing if one existed. Then it clicked! This is who you had been reminding me off. You both have those beautiful purple-blue eyes, and those eyes are what I had been seeing."

"We inherited them from our mother, and her mother. Oh, Mr. Finnigan, thank you so much for putting two and two together! You can't know how much this means to me! O.K., I'm ready for that nap now." Giving her brother a big hug, she left the room smiling.

The following few days were pure heaven for Sam. She was beside her brother every chance she got. They had many conversations trying to catch up with all the years they had been separated. Sam asked him many questions that started with 'Do you remember', but, of course, he could not answer 'Yes' to most of them.

Jeff came in one day and listened for a few minutes, then said "There are a few other questions you need to tackle as soon as possible. Such as, what do we call you? Matt is a part of your LAST name, not your given name. Would you be able to answer to Tommy or Tom now? Do you have a Birth Certificate under the name she gave you? For that matter, are any of your college credits now valid since you were not using your legal name? Unfortunately, you may not even be a State Policeman!"

"Oh, no!" Sam said. "I hadn't given a thought to all of that, but you are right! This is going to be a tangled mess to straighten out. We need to make an appointment with Jessica Davis as soon as possible!" Turning to her brother, she told him "Jessie is the attorney that worked with us when Granny Edi wanted to split up Melrose Farm and is also the one that pushed through Susan's adoption. If anyone can untangle this web, she can."

Jeff called and was able to get an appointment the very next week.

"Hello again, Dr. and Mrs. Barlow. My secretary tells me your new house is almost finished. You must be so excited!

Sam answered "Yes, we are. We are hoping to move into a section of it next week. Then I can say our baby was born in the new house. Not that she or he will care, but the idea means a great deal to Jeff and me.

"Something else that means a great deal to me, Jessie, is the mess this gentleman finds himself in, through no fault of his own. I don't know if you have heard, but this is the brother I thought was dead for about twenty years. He has many problems because of that, and we are hoping you can help him solve at least some of them."

"Oh, my! Thought dead for twenty years! Yes, I can see that might cause a few problems. Why don't we start at the beginning and try to sort this out one step at the time?"

As Matt/Tommy began the story, Jessie interrupted to ask "And you were part of an FBI search? For how long?"

"About four years." Sam said.

"That's good to know. We can subpoena those records to support your case. Please continue with your story, Mr., ah What do I call you?"

"Well, mam, that is part of the problem. I have been called Matthew or Matt all this time, but I just found out that is my LAST name. Again, I don't know exactly who I am anymore."

"I understand. How about this? So, you feel more comfortable, why don't we continue calling you Matt for this interview. We can sort out the best name later."

"That will be a relief. Thank you."

As Matt continued to explain his life in Alaska and what had happened at the State Police Convention, Jessie often asked questions and was constantly taking notes. At the end of the interview, Jessie said "Well, it seems you do have a bit of a mess to untangle. However, it may not be as difficult as it seems right now. I will immediately get in touch with the FBI for those records. I believe we can count on their full support, as they will want to truly 'close the case' for their own benefit. I would like to talk to Mrs. Cole and get her sworn statement, but I can do that over the phone. That will go a long way in proving your story. I will also contact all the schools in Alaska, from grade school to the Police Academy, to see how difficult they are going to be about re-issuing your diplomas with the correct name. I will also start the process of getting you a corrected Birth Certificate. I wo…"

"Oh, that will not be necessary Jessie. I kept his when I cleaned out the house after Daddy died." Reaching into her purse, Sam handed over a much-folded document. "It sounds silly now, but for years after Tommy disappeared, I would take this out to look at often, just to remind myself he really had existed. As you can probably guess, I adored my little brother, and his kidnapping was very hard for me to accept."

"I'm sure it must have been, but I'm glad you indulged yourself in a little bit of being silly. This original Birth Certificate is very good news, indeed! I'll keep a copy to add to the file, and you keep this original in a very safe place. Matt, I assume you had to have one under the false name to be accepted in the school systems. It would be a good idea to have a copy of that in your file here.

"Now, as I was about to say, I would recommend that you take a leave of absence from whatever State Police unit you are assigned to right now until we can get this sorted out. Legally, you are no longer a trooper, so any action you take would be illegal. You could even be arrested for "impersonating an officer of the law" if anyone wanted to get nasty about it. You may be asked to resign, then re-apply, but we can fight that if it happens. This will take some time, you understand, but I truly think we can sort all of this out with a little perseverance and patience. Are there any questions from either of you?"

There were no questions, so they all stood up and left the room. As they were leaving, Jessie said to Matt/Tommy, "I know this sounds a little melodramatic, but it would be best if you didn't leave town in the near future. The FBI may have some questions for you, and that should be done in my office. Take care and enjoy being a part of the wonderful family you are now a part of."

Getting back to Melrose Farm was accomplished in almost complete silence, except for a comment from Sam. "Somehow, I just knew Jessie would know what to do. Did you two notice how she didn't have to think about what had to be done, but just went ahead and planned how to get it done? I'm sure she will get it all straightened out very soon, Tommy."

Sam and Matt/Tommy did a lot of driving around to get him acquainted with the village, and he explored all the tunnels out to the Summer Kitchen. He felt more relaxed and completely comfortable with his 'new family'.

Things were pretty quiet for the next couple of weeks, until one night Sam shook Jeff awake and said "I think it's time to call the midwife, Jeff. Our baby is about to be born." She had decided early on that she didn't want to go to the hospital for the birth. Because she was the wife of the Chief of Staff, she was treated as Royalty and didn't care much for the honor.

After calling Mrs. Bloom, Jeff called Meli, then Katie. The family came over to the new house as a group, sitting with him in the still not quite finished living room for about sixteen hours. Then Mrs. Bloom came to the door, with Doc Simmons right behind her, to tell Jeff he could come into the bedroom to say 'Hello' to his son.

While Jeff was in the bedroom, Katie's phone rang. It was King calling his sister to let her know Abbie had just delivered his second son and Ren was ecstatic about his new baby brother. Ruth had been with her, and he had called on the same doctor that treated Meli when she first came to the Castle. She relayed the news of Sam's baby, and they celebrated together over the phone for the good news. Granny Edi was also excited about having two new babies to cuddle whenever they could all get together again.

Sam was encouraged to rest a lot for the next week, so she devoted her energy to caring for the baby and getting her new house in order. Her brother was blown away with the Crystal Cave and approved the addition of a "wall' of acrylic in front of it to keep human hands from touching the delicate crystals growing on the walls and ceiling.

"These caves and tunnels are fabulous, Sam, and I can see why you would not want to disturb them by making them part of your home. Just to have access to them any time you like is enough."

"Yes, and Si did a marvelous job of tying in some of the tunnels as hallways for the house but leaving the formations intact. And Meli loves the fact she and Katie can come see us in bad weather without even going outside.

"Speaking of them, I think I hear a lot of chatter right now. Come on in, ladies. Will you join us for a cup of coffee?"

"Yes, if I can sit at the window instead of the kitchen table. I just love this view!" Katie climbed up on a stool that stood beside a large window with a bar running the length of it. From there, almost the whole valley was visible, even the church steeple in the village.

"We came on a mission, Sam." Meli said. "Granny Edi wants to know if you and Jeff have decided on a name for that sweet boy of yours? It's time you know. You have to stop calling him "The Baby" and give the poor child a proper name!"

"Well, you can tell her we have, and planned to unveil it this evening at the family gathering. I believe my brother also has an announcement to make at that time, so you may need to bring out a peach pie to help celebrate. We'll be there at the usual time."

"O.K. then. I'll just finish my coffee and then go pull that pie out of the freezer. You know, Granny was just saying the other day we are going to have to have a pie baking day soon. According to her, we are running low on all but the mincemeat. Since that is usually saved for the Christmas season, there is still a good supply. But we are going to have to do a 'fruit buying' trip soon."

Sam's brother had been quietly drinking his coffee, but now asked a question. "I have noticed that your Granny Edi seems to know things she should not be able to because of her blindness. How can that be? For instance, how can she know how many pies of each kind are left?"

Sam laughed, then said "Amazing, isn't she? When I first came here, I was constantly startled when she would tell me things like that. Then she told me her secrete. Granny Edi grew up in that house where she is living. She knew every nook and cranny in the place. She only lost her sight after she was an adult, so the layout of the house was already a part of her everyday life. She learned to make codes for herself, such as different corners cut from the different labels for her jams and jellies, or special pie pans for the different types of fillings.

"She knows by touch what is what, and we always make sure things are put in the same place in the kitchen. When she cooks or bakes, she knows right where to go to get the sugar or flour, or even where the milk bottle is in the fridge, or where all the spices will be, in order, so she knows which is the cinnamon and which is anise. We help her, but she is very independent on her own. She raised Will from a young age despite the fact she was blind and continues to confound us at times. Now, all of you disappear. I need to go give the baby his bath."

That evening everyone was in a good mood, and anxious to hear what the baby's name would be. Jeff finally stood up, tapped his spoon on the side of his cup to get their attention.

"The moment you have all been waiting for has arrived!" Turning to where Sam sat with the baby sleeping on her shoulder he continued. "I would like to introduce Mr. Robert Dale Barlow, named after Sam's Dad and mine. We will call him Dale."

"A toast to Dale Barlow," shouted Russell. Everyone raised their coffee cup and said, "To Dale Barlow!"

Sam lowered her cup and nudged her brother with her elbow. "Your turn."

He stood and said "First, I would like to thank all of you for accepting me into this wonderful family. I know it has been difficult these last few weeks, not knowing what to call me other than "Sam's Brother", but now there is something else you can call me. Since I have found I like my original name just fine, I will now be known as Thomas Robert Matthews, Jr., and will now answer to Tom. Sorry, Sam. I just feel I've outgrown 'Tommy'! The 'Robert' part might get a little confusing with that being a part of Dale's name too, but I am very proud to share it with him. It really helps make me feel a part of the family, and I think my father would have approved. I would also like to say that having finally found my sister after all these years, I feel like I'm the luckiest man alive." And he sat down.

"A toast to Tom Matthews!" shouted Jeff. Everyone raised their cups again and said, "To Tom Matthews!"

Chapter Twenty-four

KING CALLED THE NEXT day to tell them he and Abbie had chosen the name James Winters Cole for their baby. "James is my middle name and Winters to honor her father. Not many of you will remember, but Winters was Abbie's maiden name before she married "The Creep". We will call our son James. No 'Jimmy', thank you very much. We want him to grow into 'James' and not have to grow out of 'Jimmy'. And the twins already spoil their little brother!"

When the message was relayed to the family, Tom looked at Sam and mouthed "The Creep"?"

She smiled and told him "It's a long story and I'll tell you later. Just know that Abbie is very glad he is no longer in her life, but she can't forget he was the father of her twins."

Several days later, Jeff told Sam he had a Medical Conference to attend. "But you will never guess where it is to be held. Richmond! How would you and Tom like to go with me, and we can show him your old hometown?"

"Oh, Jeff, that would be such fun! He probably will not remember much of it, but that's O.K. Just seeing it again will be interesting for me as well. Will we drive or fly down."

"I thought we could drive. That way you can have the car while I'm tied up in meetings."

"I guess we need to check with Jessie to see if it is O.K. for him to leave town. I don't want to do anything that would cause problems with his suit to get his name back. I'll call tomorrow."

Jessie gave them permission if they checked in with her every day.

They had a lovely three days. Sam drove to the street where her old house was, and Tom said he remembered playing on the front porch. She took him by his old school, but it brought back no memories at all, however, he did remember the playground and park where they used to go for picnics. Then she drove into the city and down to the street where the boarding house where she and Meli had lived after they graduated from college should have been. Unfortunately, time had taken a toll on the area and the building they had lived in was in the process of being demolished.

"Didn't you say the building Superintendent was a good friend?" Tom asked.

"Yes, she was, and we have kept in touch. Her husband was promoted about the same time they found out this old building was to be torn down, so they moved out to the suburbs to a small house with a yard. She is retired and enjoys gardening and only having her own home to clean and take care of instead of a whole apartment building."

Sam saw that the old deli had not changed, and the bookstore around the corner was still there. They brought back a lot of memories for her, but she was glad to live where she did now. The whole 'family' at Granny Edi's was very special to her, and she was very happy with the way her life had turned out. Especially now that her brother was back in her life. As they were driving around on the last day, suddenly Sam said "Would you..." At the same time Tom blurted "Could we..."

They both laughed, then Tom said "Go ahead, Sis. Ladies first."

"Well, I was about to ask if you would like to go out to the cemetery where Mom and Daddy are buried?"

"Hey! I was going to ask if we could go there! Yes, I think seeing their graves would help me heal. Let me know that they really were a part of my life. Is it far?

"No, not at all. There is a small florist shop where I always stop on the way to purchase a little something to put on the headstone. Do you mind if we stop this time? It won't take but a minute."

"That's a good idea. I'd like to add a flower or two myself."

After purchasing two small arrangements, Sam shortly pulled into the parking lot of a beautiful little church with graves all around it.

"This is where we used to go to services every Sunday. I know you probably don't remember that, but you really enjoyed your Sunday School Class, and would recite Bible verses all the way home."

"Wait! There was another boy about my age there. His name was Toby, and we would always sit together! Wow! I do remember that."

"Oh, Tommy, really? I'm so glad some of your memories are coming back. Come on, Mom and Daddy are right over here, as well as their parents. You will get to meet several of your ancestors today!"

"You're kidding! Both sets of Grandparents? SammyAnn, thank you so much for this. I'm glad you brought me here."

Tom gently placed his arrangement on the headstone for his parents, then knelt on one knee and bowed his head for a moment. Sam went over to where their Grandparents were buried, gently divided her arrangement into two smaller ones and put half on each headstone. Tom soon joined her, and they stood quietly for a few minutes, then turned as one and headed back to the car. If Sam noticed the tears in Tom's eyes, she didn't mention it.

The good weather held, so it was a pleasant drive back. Sam and Tom talked almost nonstop. Taking care of Dale's needs while riding in the back seat was a bit of a challenge but she managed.

Getting back home late in the day, Tom said he would wait and call Jessie in the morning. When he did, he came rushing into the kitchen to tell Sam and Jeff the good news.

"My schools in the small town where I grew up were most cooperative. Unknown to me at the time, the family I lived with was not well liked, and the school officials were not surprised when Miss Davis told them the circumstances. It seems they had already found out that my 'Aunt Gail' was not really a certified teacher at all, and it was her husband who had forged her credentials. He may even have been the one that forged my 'birth certificate'. Anyway, they were more than happy to send corrected copies of my diplomas and Miss Jessie has them waiting at her office. She hasn't heard anything from my college in Anchorage or the State Police Academy but will keep after them. I told her I would come pick up what she had if I could bum a ride to the right place. I haven't been here long enough to know my way around."

"I'll be happy to take you, Tom." Sam said. "Let me see if Katie or Meli need anything from the grocery store. I need to stop there anyway, so might as well get whatever they need while I'm picking up mine. Dale and I'll be ready to leave in about half an hour."

When they arrived at Jessie's office, she was delighted to learn about the decision to use 'Tom' as his name. "Having only one name to deal with will make your court case go a lot smoother.

"The FBI would like to meet you here next Tuesday at ten, if that will be good for you."

"I think I can do that. We are going by the office to get a new driver's license after leaving here. Will I need any paperwork from you?"

"Yes. I'll give you a letter explaining the matter, and you will also need to tell them to cancel your old one or you will continue to get renewal notices. Mrs. Cole sent her statement, so that is another bit of proof in your file. This is coming together very well. Now if we can just get your schools in Anchorage to answer my letters, we'd be ready for a court date."

Leaving the lawyer's office, Sam drove two blocks to the grocery store, telling Tom "You need to go just across the street, second door on the right. I'll zip in here and pick up the few things I need and meet you back here when you are finished. Then I would like to take a few minutes to run into that shop right over there. They ordered a few things for my baby's room, and I'd like to pick them up while I am in town."

"No problem. It will give me a chance to get to know your village a little better."

Errands completed; they went back to Sam's house. Jeff was still at the hospital, so they had a quick lunch and then Tom asked for some advice.

"Sam, do you know of an honest car dealership around here? I would like to have my own transportation so I'm not a burden on you."

"Tom Matthews, don't you ever think of yourself as a burden to me! I am just so happy to have you back, I'd drive you around forever. But I can see where you need to be independent. Yes, if you can wait until after Dale's nap, we'll go get a car for you. You do have some money? Or I will be honored to buy my little brother a car!"

"Not likely! I have my own money, thank you very much. Most of it is the money I got when I sold my other car just before leaving Alaska. The Police furnished a car, so I've just never bought another one. I am a little concerned now about how to earn more. If the State Police will not accept my 'claim to a different name', I'm not sure exactly what I'll do. Policework is the only thing I know."

"I'm sure it will all work out. Just don't worry about until you find out what they will want from you. I'm going to put Dale down for his nap. Why don't you relax in the living room for a while, maybe even read some of those new magazines that came yesterday. I'll be back soon."

After putting her baby down in his crib, she decided to call Abbie to see how she was getting along with her new baby.

"Sam! So good to hear from you. How wonderful that our

babies will share a birthday! Can't you just imagine Granny Edi the first time they are together?"

"Yep, she is already planning it! Hey, I want to thank you so much for sending your statement to Jessie so quickly. It really made Tom happy to know you would do that for him. I don't think he has had much support from family over the years."

"I was super glad to help. I know how much you would like to have him back, so was happy to do anything I could. How is he getting along?"

"Things are going well with getting all the evidence for his court case. He is going out to purchase a car this afternoon, and maybe even start looking for a job. The State Police Academy in Anchorage is dragging their feet about accepting his real name, so he may not be able to go back to that, at least not right away. We'll just have to wait and see. How are you managing with three babies? I now know how difficult it is with just one!"

"Everything is wonderful. Maria is such a help, and even Rona and Ren help by bring us what he needs. They like 'caring for beebee'. Oops, I spoke too soon. There seems to be an argument over who will get his bottle from the kitchen. 'Gotta go. Talk to you soon."

Abbie went to settle the argument, let one twin go get the bottle Maria had heated, then let the other twin hold it for the 'beebee', then went to knock on King's door.

When told to come on in, she said "King, weren't you telling me a couple of days ago that you guys were thinking of starting up some kind of Security Force at Clover Leaf Resort?"

"Yes, we are. Why, are you thinking to apply?"

"Cute! But no. I do have a suggestion, though. I just talked with Sam, and it appears Tom may not be able to be a State Policeman again for a long while. The Academy where he graduated does not want to accept his real name and give him another diploma. Would he have to have one from them to be on the Security Force for the Resort?"

"No, he wouldn't and thank you for the idea! Because the Resort is a privately owned company, we could hire anyone we want, even just someone off the street if we wanted to. I'll call the other two right now and get their opinion. A trained law enforcement officer would be a great asset to us."

The FBI interview was over, and they were very glad to accept the evidence to prove Tom was who he claimed to be. Since all the people involved in his kidnapping were now dead, there was no one to prosecute so they could officially close the case. The college he had graduated from accepted Jessie's evidence and issued a new diploma. The only holdout was the Police Academy. They were unwilling to issue another diploma until he went back there and completed two more years of school.

As soon as Tom heard that requirement, he talked at length with Sam to find out what he could about King and exactly what Clover Leaf Resort was. Then he called King to accept his job offer, packed up what little he owned into his new car, and drove to Texas. Tom Matthews became Head of Security for the Clover Leaf Resort and had his own office in the Business Tower with ten deputies working under him. They even had uniforms with the clover leaf logo Sam had designed. It was rather striking, with a tower drawn inside each leaf of the clover.

Chapter Twenty-five

ABOUT A WEEK AFTER Tom headed West, Jeff came into the bedroom one evening to find Sam curled into her favorite chair, crying.

"Sam?" What's wrong, honey? Is Dale alright?"

"Oh, the baby is fine. It's just losing Tom all over again! We just found each other and now he's gone halfway across the country to work. I'm so glad King offered him the job, but I just wish it weren't so far away. I just talked to him on the phone, but it's not the same. If he is happy doing what he is doing, I know I shouldn't complain, but I just wish he lived closer."

"Yeah, that's a bummer, all right. But you know he will be happy doing what he was trained for. And we can visit often. As a matter of fact, with the Holiday coming up and Doc Simmons as a backup, I can take several days off from the Hospital. How would you like to spend six days at a luxury resort?"

"Jeff! Could we really? That would be wonderful, and we can ask Abbie and King to have the holiday meal there with us and Tom. It would be the first time I have missed spending the holiday with Granny Edi, but I think she will forgive me.

Can I call Abbie right away? Maybe she can find a couple of babysitters for our four little ones for some of the time."

"Excellent idea. While you two make your plans, I'm going down to Granny Edi's house for a couple of hours. Will and Russell have challenged me to a game of Billiards and said Doc might be stopping by for a few rounds. I have a medical question I want to ask him about one of my patients, so this will be a good time. Don't wait up."

Jeff called King the next day and made reservations for his break time, and they flew out commercially to save the driving time. King had apologized for not picking them up in the corporate jet, but he had no reason to come East at the time, and they both agreed it would be foolish to do the round trip. King did pick them up at the airport in Texas and drove them down to Clover Leaf Resort. They met Kelly, then went over to the other side of the duplex and unpacked.

An hour later, Tom met them at the duplex, then they went to Megan's restaurant at the top of The Business Tower, where they met King and Abbie for lunch. Megan seated them at a large round table where they could see all the way to the Cole's cavern home almost thirty miles away.

Sam had grabbed the seat next to her brother and spent the better part of the afternoon catching up with what had been his life before Abbie recognized his story for the one she had heard many times from Sam. They also discussed his new job here at the resort, and if he was settling in, and did he like it as much as being a State Policeman.

At one point Tom said "As I told you back at Granny Edi's, I felt very lucky to have found you again after all the years apart. Now that I'm here, with even more 'family' and all the new friends I've made, I truly feel like I am the Luckiest Man Alive. I have been accepted into your extended family, and King's business partners have made me feel very welcome. I love the work even more than being with the State Police, as I learned there are just too many restrictions on their Force. Here at Clover Leaf Resort, life is a bit more relaxed and without the threat of being caught in a shootout on the street! There is very little crime here, it's mostly making sure the tourist or permeant residents don't exceed the posted speed limits, or helping someone find what they are looking for, or helping someone change a tire on the way out to the airstrip. I've even taken up gulf! So, yes, SammyAnn, life is good."

"I'm so glad you feel that way. I just wish you could have found this happiness closer to me!"

Abbie spoke up from the other side of Tom. "But having him here gives King even more of an excuse to fly that plane! Did you know he is planning to put in a runway right next to The Castle, and has almost talked Russell into putting in one in the meadow next to the barn at Granny Edi's? 'That will save us so much time by not having to drive out to the airport at either end.' he tells me! Russell is dragging his feet though. He is afraid of what it will do to Granny's goats. And speaking of the goats, I need to talk to you, Sam. I got a call from our manager at the Phoenix Fabrics mill yesterday. He would like to talk to one of us at the mill soon about the fabrics he is producing for us.

"Jeff and I could probably stop by there on our way home. Is there a problem?"

"I don't think so. More like not enough business. I think he wants to expand the selection to have more designs, and since that is your job, I'm glad for you to handle it."

Tom spoke up to say, "Maybe I missed something, but what is Phoenix Fabrics?"

"Ah, another one of those "family things' you haven't been back long enough to learn about." Sam said. "You see, when Abbie first came to live with the Melrose Farm family, she made her living sewing costumes for Riverboat shows on the Mississippi, and other period venues that needed turn of the century costumes. She was beginning to find it difficult to find the particular fabric designs she liked, so I began drawing them for her. Then we had the good fortune to hear of a fabric mill for sale, so bought it, changed the name, and now produce our own fabric."

"And now it looks as if that may be changing again. My customer base is shrinking, as more of the Riverboats are going with the modern "New York Stage" type shows, so don't want period costumes anymore. Their shows now have professional companies that furnish all the costumes as a package when they buy the rights to produce the shows. The "Old Southern Plantations" still buy from me, but that will not pay enough for me to even stay in business. Which isn't really a problem anymore, now that my wonderful husband has vowed to take care of me "till death do us part". But I would still like to have a way to contribute my share."

Chapter Twenty-six

ᴍ ᴇɢᴀɴ ᴄᴀᴍᴇ ᴀɴᴅ sᴀᴛ with them for a half hour or so,
then they broke up so those not on vacation could get
back to work, while Sam, Jeff and Abbie found one of the
gulf carts and took a tour of the resort. Abbie was very proud
of what her husband and his partners had built here and was
happy to show it off. The tour was cut short when first one,
then all the other babies began to let it be known they were
needing a nap. Abbie dropped Sam and her family off at the
duplex, then took the gulf cart back, left it in a parking space,
then went up to King's office. He had reserved the apartment
right next door for when he and his family wanted a weekend
away. Abbie took the babies there, settled them down for a
nap, then settled down in a comfortable chair with a book.
She wasn't there long before she began to nod off. Handling
all three children without the help of Maria was difficult and
she was a bit worn out.

King came in and woke her up in time to get everyone
ready for the special dinner Megan was hosting, with everyone
invited including Kelly. When they arrived at the Tower
Restaurant, they were shown directly to the Starlight Lounge.
Tom had picked up his sister and her family, so they were

already there when the Cole's arrived. Bill Travis and Gordan Granger arrived separately a little later, Kelly walking shyly slightly behind Gordan.

"Whose idea was this lounge?" Sam wanted to know. "It is magnificent! The view of the river is wonderful and there really is starlight!"

"Actually, I give all the credit to Katie!" Megan said. "She suggested rooftop seating for One Hundred and One, so I thought it might work here as well." Raising her voice to be heard over the chatter, she said "All of you, help yourselves to the food on the table over there, and one of the wait staff will be in soon to take your main course orders." Turning to Sam she said "So having Tom turn up after being gone so long must have been a shock. And you had no idea where he was all these years?"

"No, we didn't. The FBI told us they must be dead, as the trail just ended. Thanks to yet another change of names, looks, and clothing, that woman was able to pass him off as her daughter and slip through the net. That must have been when she was able to get both of them all the way to the last end of nowhere in Alaska."

"The Aleutian Islands! I have always wanted to go there. It sounds so romantic to live so close to another country. Tom, did you know any Russians?"

"Yes, I did. There were several second and third generation 'Ruskies' in my grade in school, and I learned to speak their language almost as well as English. I also learned a good bit of the local native 'Eskimo' language."

"That must have been an exciting time for you."

"Well, I don't think 'exciting' is really the correct word. It was just my life as I knew it. I only started questioning those things after I moved to Anchorage. But I can tell you one thing. I never felt as at home there as I have since finding my big sister and her extended family. Did you know, Granny Edi even called me "Grandson" just before I left to come out here? I never had a grandparent before!"

Sam said "Well, actually you did, of course, but all but Daddy's mother had passed before you were born. She even lived with us for a few years, and I have pictures somewhere of her holding you in her lap. Jeff, please remind me when we get home. I'll dig them out and send you copies. As for Granny Edi, that wonderful lady made all of us feel right 'at home' from the very beginning. I'm glad she has included you in that. Now, Megan, is this Prime Rib Dinner as good as it sounds?"

"Ah, Sam, you must know I only use the best beef Daddy can raise for both of my restaurants. I dare you to find any better even in those fancy places back East."

"Then that's what I'll have. How about you, Jeff?"

"Sounds good to me!"

As it did to most of them, so the ordering went quickly.

Abbie was settled next to Sam, and had just slathered her baked potato with a pound of butter, when Sam asked "About Phoenix Fabrics? What is he looking for exactly? You said something about increasing the line, but does that mean more designs from me?"

"I'm not sure. He may mean adding entirely different designs to go after a different market. I have convinced King to add a "Sewing Shop" here in the Business Tower, so have been talking to a woman who can manage it. She says fabrics for quilting are now all 'the thing' as she puts it, and they are mostly geometrics or florals. Your small-scale motifs we use for the period dresses are used also, but not as much."

King spoke up to say, "You know that whatever fabrics you ladies produce in your mill will be stocked in the shop here, so if it means different designs, make them something these Western ladies will want in their quilts."

"Good point, King. I guess I'm just going to have to wait until I meet with him to see what I need to do. Now, tell me what you have planned for tomorrow to show off your Resort."

Bill answered from across the table "Fishing!"

"Fishing?"

"Yep. Gordon and I are going to take you upriver in one of the Resort boats for a bit of Catfish sport. Abbie and Kelly will take all the babies, so you will not have to worry about your son falling overboard, and Megan will cook our catch for dinner. If we catch anything. If we don't, we can still have a good meal right here. But it means getting an early start! You will have to be at the dock by eight o'clock. Kelly is coming in early to be there for Dale. I've even given your brother the day off so he can come with us."

"Oh, that does sound like fun! I hope I haven't forgotten how. It has been a very long time since I've held a fishing rod in my hands. Tom, do you remember Daddy taking us fishing on the lake back home? You were very small, so maybe not."

"No, I don't remember that at all. Maybe going out tomorrow, some of it will come back to me. It should be fun anyway."

Chapter Twenty-seven

Tom was already at the pier when they got there the next morning. Jeff laughed and said "You're here early! Anxious to catch some fish, Tom?"

Tom just smiled and looked at Sam, then burst into song "We're goin' to tha' lake and we're gonna catch our dinner. We're goin' to tha lake to see who's tha best swimmer!"

"Oh, Tommy, you do remember!"

"Well, some of it anyway and that was still off-key just like it used to be. It was Dog Leg Lake, and I always asked, 'Where is the rest of the dog?' It all just came back to me as I was getting dressed this morning, 'cause I was 'goin' to tha' lake'! Well, river actually, but it did bring back some good memories."

"That's wonderful! I am so glad you are remembering things."

Gordan asked "Why did you think you didn't remember anything?"

"To quote Abbie, 'THAT woman', as she calls the woman I thought was my mother all these years, would not let me remember things. Every time I said something about my family, or my house, or my school, she would tell me it was all a bed dream and I had to not think about those things. Over time, I stopped talking about them, but I guess I never really forgot any of it."

"You were also very young when she took you, so it is natural for you not to remember much about that time." Sam said. "Not many people remember things that happened before they were four or five years old!"

"I guess that's true. Now let's go see if I remember how Daddy taught me to bait a hook! He did try to teach me, right?"

"He did. You were a quick learner for someone so young, and he told you so."

"I remember him saying that! I strutted around for a week afterward. Golly, gee whiz!"

"And you said THAT all the time too! Something you learned from another little boy on our block."

Bill said "O.K. Enough chit-chat. Into the boat. Now, you've got me wondering if you can bait a hook!"

He could and ended up catching more than anyone else.

The fishing trip was a huge success, with Sam and Jeff both catching two, they all enjoyed a wonderful dinner of fried catfish and fresh vegetables sautéed lightly in olive oil, with a delicious four-layer chocolate cake for dessert. Sam and Tom sat as close as possible, as if they both knew this would be their last dinner together for some time. She and Jeff needed to fly out early the next day to give her time to meet with the manager of Phoenix Fabrics. Jeff, his sister, and King seemed to understand, and did not try to engage them in conversation.

"Oh, Tommy, I'm so glad we had these few days together. Please promise me you will come see us as soon as you can get some time off."

"You do know you are the only one allowed to call me "Tommy". Bill and Gordan would laugh me out of the resort if they heard you!"

"I doubt that! They seem like they are very nice people, so I'm sure they would never laugh at you. But seriously, do come to see us soon. Our house isn't quite finished, so there is no guest room yet, but you know you would be welcome at Granny Edi's, or even with Katie and Russell. Do say you'll come."

"I'm not due for any time off for the next few months, but I promise, I will not let a long time go by without seeing you. We wasted too many years away from each other to let that happen. Please tell Mr. Finnigan how much I appreciate his persistence in helping me find you. Speaking of him reminds me. Now that I'm settled here, I would like to get one of Katie's dogs for myself. I was very impressed with their work at the convention and think one might be beneficial to my work here. Lost children or hikers are bound to come up sooner or later. Besides, I just like the breed. I would enjoy having one as a companion even if I never need it on the job."

Of course, that brought more tears and more hugs, and then the party broke up. Jeff and his family left early the next day, flew about an hour, then landed again, rented a car, and drove out to the Phoenix Fabric Mill.

Jeff took his son to the nearby park while Sam went into the office building. Walking up to the lady at a big desk in the center of the room she said "Hello. My name is Samantha Barlow. I would like to see Mr. Colby, please."

"I'm sorry, but Mr. Colby isn't seeing anyone today. Would you like to make an appointment for some time next week?"

"No, I would like to see him today. You may tell him Mrs. Samantha Barlow is here. I believe that will change his mind about seeing me as soon as he's free."

"Oh, but you don't understand, Mrs. Barlow. He isn't seeing anyone today."

"Not even one of the owners of this mill?"

"What? Oh, dear me! One of the owners! Oh, my! Yes, please come with me. I'll show you right in."

As she opened the door to an inner office, she practically shouted "Mrs. Samantha Barlow is here to see you, Mr. Colby. Put in your hearing aids."

As Mr. Colby fumbled in his desk drawer to find his hearing aids, a much younger man came forward and held out his hand to shake Sam's.

"Hello. I am also Mr. Colby, this gentleman's grandson. Mrs. Barlow? One of the co-owners of this mill if I'm not mistaken."

"Yes, you are correct. What has happened here? I don't remember your grandfather being so deaf when I interviewed him for this job."

"And you would also be correct. This is something that has come about within the last six months or so. We kept telling him to wear the ear protectors when he was down on the floor, but he just would not bother. Now, he is paying the price. All that noise from the machines is slowly making him deaf. I believe he contacted Mrs. Cole recently about cutting back on the amount of fabric produced here, thinking that would help his hearing improve. It would not. Now that the damage has been done, nothing will bring it back."

"Cutting back? We thought he meant to add more. How will this affect our business, Mr. Colby? Are you telling me the mill will not be wanting to produce as many bolts of fabric for us?"

"Well, that was Gramp's idea. However, if you would be interested in an alternative plan, I believe it would benefit both of us."

"I'm all ears. Whatever will help our mill is of interest to me."

"My Grandmother and I agree we would like to see him retire, and they could then move to Florida where their three other children live. With your and Mrs. Cole's permission, my dad and I could take over this mill and continue just as before. Maybe even add to the line."

"I do like the sound of your alternative plan, Mr. Colby. I would need to speak with your father and, of course, Mrs. Cole before anything is settled. In the meantime, is there anything we can do to help your grandfather?"

"Young lady, you gave me a job when everyone else said I was too old and that is more than enough." Having gotten the aids in place, the elderly Mr. Colby now added to the conversation. "I guess I really was too old to listen to the young ones when they warned me to wear those confounded ear protectors. I thought they were being overbearing and just liked to tell me what to do. Now I realize they really knew what they were talking about. Being around all those loud weaving machines damaged my ears to the point I now need these confounded hearing aids. Now my wife tells me she wants to go live close to all those confounded grandchildren in Florida. If I decide to do that, I want you to know my son and grandson will look after this mill as if it were their own. Confound it, Bert, go tell Carol to page the floor and tell your father to get up here. He needs to talk with Mrs. Barlow."

"Yes, sir. Mrs. Barlow, would you like a cup of coffee while we wait?"

"That would be lovely, Thank you."

Bert came back in almost immediately carrying a tray with the coffee and a plate of cookies, followed by his father.

"Carol had already paged Dad and fixed up this tray by the time I got out there. She is a wonder when it comes to anticipating what will be needed. She also wants to apologize to you, Mrs. Barlow. She knew Gramps isn't comfortable seeing people anymore since he can't hear them too well even with the aids, so she tries to keep his appointments to a minimum. She didn't mean to be rude."

"She is forgiven. She was just trying to protect her boss and I admire that. So, tell me, are all three of you comfortable with this changeover? I mean, do you all agree this is what you want to do?"

The 'middle' Mr. Colby said "If it is agreeable with you and Mrs. Cole, Bert and I can take over at once. Dad has been training me to manage the floor since I was a teenager, and my son just graduated from college with a degree in business administration. We can help you build up this mill to be one of the best in the country."

"Then I have no complaints, and I can't think Mrs. Cole will mind either. We will have to draw up a different contract, of course, but there should be no problem there."

"All right! If all you young people agree, confound it, I'm going home and start packing for Florida." Grabbing the hearing aids out of his ears and shouting as he was going out the door, he said "Hazel, call my wife and tell her to meet me at the deli and I'll buy her a lemonade."

As Sam just sat staring at the door, Burt exclaimed "Well, that was to be expected! I think he has been looking for an excuse to slow down for a long time but didn't want to admit he was getting old. Dad, did you want to talk to Mrs. Barlow about our other ideas?"

"Well, I suppose we should get everything out right at the beginning. My name is Cecil Colby by the way, and together with my son, we have a few suggestions on how we can improve your fabric mill."

"As I told your son, I will be happy to listen to anything that will improve our business, Mr. Colby. What do you have in mind?

"My son tells me his studies at the university show that a business needs to diversify if they mean to make a dent in the business world. In other words, this mill, focusing on just the small designs suitable for the Period Costumes Mrs. Cole makes are not enough to make a good profit for you. You need to also have several different designs, more modern patterns suitable for the clothing of today and for the quilting craze now going on. We should also investigate not only weaving in the design but printing it on as well. That will take some capital to be sure, but the returns would soon cover the expense of the new equipment. We have drawn up some proposals we would be happy to share with you and Mrs. Cole before any decision must be made. My son also has a suggestion that will also be a major decision for you ladies. Burt?

"Ah, yes, Mrs. Barlow." Clearing his throat, he began. "As you well know, this mill is old and most of the machinery is getting old. I believe you were aware of that when you were able to purchase it at a very reduced rate. The annual repairs on the building itself and the repairs and new parts for the machines are really beginning to eat into the profits. It is our belief we should consider a new location and build a more modern facility. One closer to our thread source if possible. It seems a bit silly to pay to have the thread shipped here from the factory in the east, weave the thread into fabric, then pay to ship those bolts of fabric back to Pins 'N Needles in your hometown in the east. The fabric goes to other locations of course, but you see what I mean? This would be a major expense, but one my father and I would like to share. In other words, we would very much like to buy into your mill operation. If you and/or Mrs. Cole disagree with any of this, just say so, and things can go on as usual."

"Oh, my! This is very unexpected. So many shocks in one day, it's hard to comprehend. I will have to talk all of this over with my partner before I can give you any answers. In the meantime, can you just carry on as usual, and I will get back to you as soon as I've discussed all of this with Mrs. Cole?"

Cecil Colby said "We can, and we will do that. We just want you to know we believe this mill has a lot of potential and are willing to invest in it to see that happen. I'll get that proposal for you."

Burt rose when Sam did and said "I'll walk you out. Let me just add that what little dealings I've had with you and Mrs. Cole over the telephone, and from talking with Gramps, I believe both of you are very business-oriented ladies, and Dad and I would be proud to be a small part of what you are trying to build with Phoenix Fabrics."

When Jeff saw Sam coming out of the building, he quickly got out of the car to run and grab her hands. "Sam! Are you O.K.? You look like you are in shock. What's wrong?"

"Oh, Jeff, I am in shock, but it's in a good way, I think. Give me a few minutes to think. When does our plane leave? Why don't we just drive on out to the airport and I'll fill you in on the trip home? How was our boy? Did he like the playground at the park? He must have worn himself out. He is sound asleep!"

Chapter Twenty-eight

AFTER DISCUSSING THE SITUATION with Jeff on the plane, Sam was anxious to get home so she could call Abbie. Russell picked them up at the airport, so she launched right in to asking him about a new mill.

"It all depends on how much you and Abbie want to upgrade. I have heard those dying systems can get very expensive. And, how much your Misters Colby want to invest. Talk it over with Abbie, then see if you want to go ahead with the move. There is plenty of space out in the new Industrial Park being put in near the dam. King and I could put up a nice office building for you, but neither of us know much about factory floor layouts. You might need to call in other experts for that."

Sam could hardly wait for Jeff to open the door to the house so she and the baby could get into the kitchen. Hurrying into Dale's room, she quickly changed him and put him down in his crib. He took a deep sigh and fell asleep at once. It was as if he knew he was home and very happy about that fact.

She went back into the kitchen, thanked Jeff for starting a pot of coffee, poured herself a cup and sat down to call Abbie. An hour later, and several repeats of her conversation with the

Colbys, she hung up and went to find Jeff. Locating him in his office, she told him that Abbie was very excited about the whole idea and would plan a trip East so they could work out the details.

Sam spent every minute she could in her Graphic Arts studio. She had a couple of client jobs needing to be finished, and she was also experimenting with new patterns. On her next trip into the village for groceries, she stopped in at Pins 'N Needles to check out what was being sold there for the quilting hobbyist.

King, Abbie, all three children, and the two Colbys arrived a few days later. The Coles went directly to their apartment above the Cole, Mayhew offices, and the Colbys were shown to the guest rooms at Granny Edi's.

The next day, Sam drove Abbie and the two gentlemen out to look at the new Industrial Park. Meli, Katie, and Granny Edi were caring for all the babies in various play pens and cribs set up in the family room. Granny Edi was enjoying the experience of holding one baby, then another. Susan and the twins were getting to the age where they didn't want to sit still for long, but Granny held on as long as they would let her.

The Colby men were very interested in the area, liked the little village, and especially liked the new Industrial Park, and were happy to learn the mill that spun the thread they used was only about ten miles away. She told them what Russell had said about building a nice office building but knowing nothing about layouts for weaving mills. They assured her they could get all the drawings necessary and would pay for the building themselves as a part of their investment.

After leaving the Park, she took them to the village for their appointment with Jessica Davis to work out the business agreement. Since that took up most of the afternoon, they were glad when Meli called to let them know she and Katie had dinner almost ready.

Sam said "Oh, I am so glad. I just do not feel like fixing a meal right now."

When they arrived back at the farmhouse, they immediately were told to wash their hands and sit down. They had just about finished eating when Jude ran in to interrupt them to say one of the goats was hurt. Russell ran out to see to the animal, with Sam right behind him.

Cecil Colby said "Goats?"

Abbie answered to tell him about Granny's goat herd, and the beautiful yarn she sold at Pins 'N Needles. They were very interested, and Burt suggested Phoenix Fabrics might think about offering a line of wool fabric as well as their usual cotton.

"We would never have enough yarn for that!" Granny said. "My goats only produce enough wool for about fifty skeins per year."

Bert continued "I mean, we could purchase the wool from a commercial distributer. It would be to our advantage to offer another choice of fabric materials. As I told Mrs. Barlow earlier, we should also consider screen printing as well as woven designs for the muslin fabric, and a few bigger design images."

Sam and Russell came back in shaking their heads. Sam told them "It was just old Juno and another disagreement with Clancy." She turned to the guest to add "Juno the goat and

Clancy the rooster have never gotten along. One or the other usually ends up with an injury or two. This time Juno got the worst of it, and now has a spur cut over his left eye. We put salve on it, so it should be as good as new in a couple of days. Just in time for them to pick another fight with each other!"

The next day, Sam went out to the pasture to check on Juno and found him to be very much better. However, she noticed something else and went into the house to talk to Granny Edi.

"Granny, Juno is fine, but do you realize just how old some of your goats are getting? A couple of them are not growing the thick fleece they usually do, and one or two don't seem to be moving around as quickly as they used to. Do you want to think about replacing them to keep up the herd?"

"Sam, it's not only my goats that are getting old! I am beginning to feel older every day, and really, I don't have a need to continue keeping the goats to stay busy, which as you know, is why Will gave them to me in the first place. You and Russell have done all the work needed for the business anyway, so getting rid of them will free up your time. You do have that wonderful son now to demand you attention. Why don't you and Russell try to find someone to buy the whole herd? We may have to have the really old ones put down, but someone may want the others."

"Are you sure about this, Granny? You've had them so long, it will not seem normal around here to not hear them baaaing about the place!"

"Yes, I'm sure. I have been thinking about it for some time but just put it off. Try to get them sold before sheering time, will you? Russell just doesn't have time to deal with that anymore."

"Well, if you're sure, I'll go find Russell now."

It was a great relief to Russell to sell the goats, although he was a little sad to see them go. They had been his main job when he first came to work at Melrose Farm, and he had become fond of the silly creatures. However, his contracting business was growing well, so he did sometimes resent the time it took to care for them and get the sheering done when needed. When he gave the check for their sale to Granny Edi, they both shed a few tears.

The Colby gentlemen were given a tour of the tunnel system out to The Summer Kitchen, and then the other way to Sam's new home. She also took them on another tour of the area, even driving over into the next valley to show them the University and out to the lake to show off the Bradley Place Retirement Home. Abbie was delighted to see Mrs. Granger again, even though it did bring back bad memories of her first husband. They visited with Uncle George for a while and learned that he had almost finished writing up the history of the tunnels and caves on Melrose Farm. Burt said that he would surely purchase a copy as he had been fascinated by the tunnel system when Will took him in. After visiting with Doc Simmons, they went back to the farm for a delicious dinner prepared by Meli, with help from Granny Edi.

Sam had told Katie about her brother wanting a dog and Katie was very excited. She said "I have just the perfect one for him! She isn't as dark as my other ones. More of a yellow than golden, but she is a sweetheart. I have been calling her Rose because she reminds me of the rose growing on that trellis by the garage. If he keeps the name, he will have his very own 'Yellow Rose of Texas'!"

"Oh, you are so funny! I'll tell him what you said."

"Fine. I'll go look up a crate so King can tie her down in the plane. They are planning to leave tomorrow, you know."

The Colbys went back home to settle their affairs, and Russell drew up the plans for a modern office building. Getting both Sam and Abbie to approve it, he started the building process. Having the Faxed plans for the weaving floor from Burt, he was able to build that section as well. Burt was in the process of buying some new equipment and having it sent to the site. Pretty soon, Phoenix Fabrics was up and running in the new location. Both Colbys even had Russell's company build each of them a home in one of the subdivisions just outside the village.

As the wife of the Chief of Staff, Sam had several obligations at or for the hospital in the following couple of weeks. She also went to check on the residence for visiting parents whose child was a patient in the new Children's Wing. All was running smoothly there, and the staff lived up to their promise to keep it clean and in good repair. She was told there had been over fifty parents taking advantage of the home away from home since it opened. She also learned the washing machine was not working as well as it used to. Being used more than when the building was a private home, she could understand why it was wearing out. She made a mental note to have a heavy-duty machine sent up right away.

Si was able to finish her new home on the mountain, taking special care of the "Crystal Room". The plexiglass barrier wall in front of the beautiful crystals covering most of the natural stone walls went up with no cracks and Sam was able to breathe a sigh of relief to know the natural formation was protected. Although they seldom went in there, they took a great deal of pleasure just looking around whenever they did go in. The room was also a necessary stop for any visitors to the house.

Sam began experimenting with some larger patterns for the cotton muslin, and even drew up some she thought would be liked by those ladies in Texas. They began to produce bolts of 'dressmaking fabric' other than just Abbie's requirements for her Period costume business. Pins 'N Needles bought bolts of everything they produced, as well as the shop in the Business Tower at the Resort. Burt's wife was excellent at scouting out other fabric shops across the country, and soon they were shipping to every state.

Sam's life settled into a regular routine of taking care of her son, acting as hostess for hospital functions, going out to the mill often, drawing up new patterns for them and keeping up with her other Graphic Arts clients. Her life was very busy, and she loved every minute of it. She sometimes thought about what had brought her to this point and would smile whenever she did. How could she have known that a broken engagement, getting lost in a rainstorm, and her car sliding into a ditch would bring her so much joy!

Printed in the United States
by Baker & Taylor Publisher Services